Come CLOSER

Brenda Rothert

Cover Designer and Photographer
Sara Eirew
www.saraeirew.com

Editor
Lisa Hollett, Silently Correcting Your Grammar

Copy Editor
Taylor Bellitto

Proofreader
Joanne Thompson

Interior Design and Formatting
Christine Borgford, Type A Formatting
www.typeAformatting.com

Come
CLOSER

Chapter
ONE

I THINK IT'S the silence that wakes me up. After two weeks of sleeping in the forest, being lulled awake every morning by calling birds, running streams, and leaves dancing in the breeze, the quiet in my cabin doesn't feel right.

It's about time to get up anyway. I have to return to reality today. There were moments during the fourteen days I just spent in the Montana forest when I considered not returning. I had everything I needed to get by in a pack on my back. I considered building myself a small shelter and becoming a true mountain man. I'd spend my days fishing, hunting, and climbing. It would be a life without worry.

But my daydreams of escaping real life were interrupted every time by thoughts of my patients. I took an oath to do no harm, and I knew I couldn't uphold it and willfully leave people with serious mental illnesses.

No, I'm not the only doctor who can treat them, but I'm one of the few willing to live in rural Montana and work at Hawthorne Hill Mental Hospital. Other than a small town a few miles away, this place is isolated from civilization.

Not that you'd know it when you're on the property. Henry Hawthorne poured proceeds from his oil empire into this place back in the 1930s, and his estate provides for its upkeep.

Even the cabin I live in as a staffer at Hawthorne is nicer than any place I've lived before. I cook the fish I catch on weekends in a gourmet kitchen and write up patient reports on a leather sofa in front of a giant stone fireplace in the great room.

I walk into the bathroom and turn on the shower, then step in front of the sink while I wait for the water to get hot.

Damn. I look grizzly. The dark beard I grew while off work is almost an inch long, and my hair is wild and unwashed. I turn my face from side to side, considering keeping the beard. Maybe if it was trimmed and my hair was under control . . . ?

No. With my six-foot-five-inch height and wide frame, I already intimidate most new patients when they meet me. And the nurses like to call me Dr. Lumberjack—they'd have a field day with a beard.

I shave, shower, and dress in a flannel, jeans, and hiking boots, then make the quarter-mile walk uphill to the main Hawthorne building. I always walk to work unless there's snow on the ground, and on those days, I take a snowmobile.

Hawthorne is an inpatient mental hospital, but it looks like a luxurious hunting lodge. It's a massive log structure with private patient rooms, a library, and a two-story great room. It has thirty-eight patient rooms, which are always full. This is where the well off send their loved ones for mental help. Some patients are here short-term, and others live here for decades.

When I walk through the back entrance and go into my office, I'm surrounded by the cedar log smell of Hawthorne Hill. Written reports are stacked on my desk. I'll go through them later. I'm anxious to round on patients now. I take my white coat from a hook by the door and put it on as I walk toward the medical wing.

"Dr. Delgado, you're back." The female voice is eager and breathy. It has to be Sara.

"I am," I say, glancing over my shoulder.

"How was your vacation?"

"It was good."

"We missed you." She licks her lips and takes a step closer to me.

I don't mix business and pleasure by dating my coworkers. But if I did, Sara would be all too willing to keep my bed warm. She makes no secret of it either.

"So what's new here?" I ask. "How's Leonard?"

Sara arches her brows and shrugs. "It's hard to say. Dr. Tillman has him sedated."

"Sedated? Why?"

"He scared the life out of the new girl in Housekeeping. Told her someone had opened fire in the dining room and killed everyone."

"That's Leonard, though. He says things like that all the time."

"The new girl didn't know that. She called 911 and was hiding in a broom closet with Leonard for almost an hour until the cops found them. We had to evacuate and everything."

I sigh heavily. "I still don't see why Tillman sedated Leonard over that. This is a mental hospital, for Christ's sake."

"He just restrained him at first, but Leonard was a wreck. He just sobbed nonstop."

"He has a fear of being restrained. Didn't anyone tell Tillman?"

Sara nods. "It didn't help. You know how he is."

"Shit." I shake my head in disgust. "That wouldn't have happened if I'd been here."

"You can't work three hundred sixty-five days a year, Dr. Delgado." Sara gives me an admonishing look. "Oh, and we filled Nicole's bed the day after she was discharged."

"Oh, yeah?"

Sara and I walk toward the coffeemaker while talking, and I pour myself a cup.

"The new patient's name is Allison. She's been here for ten days and hasn't said a word," Sara says, pouring herself a cup of coffee, too.

"Catatonic?"

"No. She was strangled, so her vocal cords may have been damaged. Or it could be shock. She witnessed her sister's murder."

"Oh, shit. That's terrible."

Sara's gaze is sympathetic. "Wait till you read her report."

"Yeah, I think I'll go read it before I round so I'm ready to see her. How's she doing here so far?"

Sara shrugs. "Hard to say. Tillman has her sedated."

I'm gritting my teeth so hard I feel them grinding. It's all I can do to stay professional right now.

"Tell him to find me before he leaves, please," I say to Sara.

"Yes, Dr. Delgado."

There's some stomp in my step as I walk back to my office. This is why I was hesitant to take two weeks off—because putting the care of my patients in someone else's hands is a hard thing to do. But it should have been safe to leave Brody Tillman in charge. He works under me three days a week and covers me on weekends and days off. He knows damn well how I want patients treated.

When I get to my office, I close the door and sink down into my leather desk chair. I know I need to listen to Tillman before jumping his ass, but it'll be hard. And all I can do at this point is write him up and tell him I expect better next time.

Dwelling on things that can't be undone is my Achilles' heel. It's how I got into such a bad place that I needed two weeks away from here. I was about to drown my pain in a bottle of Jack, and with me, it never stops at just one. I worked too hard for my sobriety to risk losing it, so I had to get my ass to a place where I could reset my mind.

The unfamiliar name on the file at the top of the pile on my desk catches my eye.

Allison Cole

I open the folder, put on my reading glasses and dig into the report on Hawthorne Hill's newest patient.

Patient: Allison Cole

Age: 27

Sex: F

Residence: 427 Parkland Ave., Apt. 2, Chicago

Summary: Cole was admitted to Hawthorne Hill on 3/25/2016 by her aunt, Margaret Cole. Margaret Cole reports her niece was in good health physically and mentally before 3/16/2016, when she witnessed the death of her sister, Ava Cole.

According to police reports from the Chicago Police Department, Allison Cole was present at Ava Cole's apartment when armed assailants bound and gagged both women and cut Ava Cole's throat. Police have no suspects in the murder.

Neighbors of Ava Cole reported to police sounds of a struggle in her apartment. There was no sign of forced entry. Police discovered Ava Cole's body upon their arrival. Allison Cole showed physical signs of strangulation. She was inconsolably upset but would not respond to police questioning. Margaret Cole reports she picked Allison up from the police station and took her back to her home in Manhattan, where they stayed for three days. When Allison still hadn't spoken in that time, Margaret Cole took her to see her physician, Dr. Jill Warner, and psychiatrist, Dr. Li Ching. Warner and Ching advised Margaret Cole that her niece may need time to recover from the trauma she witnessed. Margaret Cole said she was worried her niece may harm herself, and she was unable to watch her around the clock. She requested a referral to an inpatient facility from Warner. Warner called Hawthorne Hill administration on 3/24/2016 and received approval for referral.

Hawthorne Hill staff assessed Allison Cole upon admission. She was physically well, though dehydrated. Dr. Brody Tillman prescribed IV hydration. Allison Cole pulled out her IV multiple times before being restrained.

Update: 3/27/2016—Hawthorne Hill psychiatrist Dr. Marcia Heaton held a session with patient Cole. Cole did not respond to questions by Heaton.

Update: 4/1/2016—Hawthorne Hill psychiatrist Dr. Marcia Heaton held a session with patient Cole. Cole did not respond to questions by Heaton.

Update: 4/2/2016—Hawthorne Hill psychiatrist Dr. Marcia Heaton held a session with patient Cole. Cole did not respond to questions by Heaton.

Update: 4/5/2016—Hawthorne Hill psychiatrist Dr. Marcia Heaton held a session with patient Cole. Cole did not respond to questions by Heaton.

I close the file and exhale deeply. Heaton thinks she has a soft touch, but not so much. She graduated at the top of her medical school class, but I think she chose the wrong specialty. She expects constant, measurable improvement from patients because it makes her feel like a success. But some people here will never recover to the point of returning to society. I don't believe in pushing my patients. My job is to support them. They need a safe place, safe people to talk to if they want to, and control over as many things as we can safely give them control over.

Allison Cole's story is still running through my mind on the walk to Leonard's room. I don't have a favorite patient, but if I did . . . what the hell, I *do*, and it's Leonard. He's a sixty-one-year-old black man with a gray beard and a head full of conspiracy theories. But he's also sharp and observant—something many people don't notice because of his paranoia.

When I see Leonard's arms and feet restrained to the safety bars on his bed, I sigh softly. I'd go several rounds with Tillman right now if he weren't such a pansy. The guy deserves to have the smug look wiped off his pretty face.

Leonard's no threat to anyone. I walk out of his room and grab the chart hanging next to his door, noting my order for an immediate removal from sedation. I'll come by and see him later, when he's awake.

I look in on a few other patients before arriving at Allison Cole's room. Like Leonard, she's bound to the bed with restraints, and she appears to be sleeping.

She looks fragile. It's not just her petite frame, but also the shadows under her eyes. Her dark brown hair hangs loosely over her shoulders, its shine telling me it was washed recently.

Our nursing aides are devoted to the patients. I noticed the difference in approach immediately when I came to Hawthorne Hill after only working at big, metropolitan hospitals. Not that the staff at large hospitals aren't devoted, because they are. But at Hawthorne, we know the patients well. We see them for days, months, even years on end.

That may be why I have such a fondness for Leonard. I've been at Hawthorne for a little over a year, and he's been here since before I started. For me, the place wouldn't be the same without him.

I take a final look at Allison and almost remove her restraints. How many fucking times have I told Tillman that restraining a sedated patient is overkill?

But since I'm taking her off sedation and she's pulled out her IV lines before, I leave her restrained. I mark her chart to stop administering the sedative, looking up from what I'm writing when I hear a howling sound.

We're in rural Montana, but I know there's not a wolf on the loose in Hawthorne. The howl came from the pediatric wing, and it sounded just like Billy McGrath. Billy has multiple personalities, and some of them aren't human.

I tuck my pen into the pocket of my white coat and head toward the howl.

Chapter
TWO

THE SCENT OF cedar is lulling me to go somewhere. I follow the sweet, clean smell, trying to open my eyes so I can figure out where I'm going. My eyelids are so heavy, though.

I turn my head to the side, still trying to open my eyes. There's something I don't like about not being able to see what's happening around me, but I can't quite remember what it is. This sense of being underwater seems impossible to shake.

Might as well just sink back into the dark, murky depths of the ocean inside my head. It's too hard to find the water's surface.

"Allison?"

The sound of the deep, unfamiliar male voice forces me out of my slumber. When I open my eyes, there's a tall man in a white coat standing several feet from me.

My heart flies into overdrive. I try to move away from him, but my hands hardly move. I'm tied to the sides of a bed.

It comes back in an instant. I'm at Hawthorne Hill, the mental hospital in Montana that Aunt Maggie dumped me off at. But who is the dark-haired man in my room?

"You're safe, Allison," he says, putting his hands out in front of his chest to show me they're empty.

Like that helps. This guy could kill me with one of his bear-paw-sized hands wrapped behind his back. I jerk against the restraints, tears filling my eyes.

"I'm Daniel Delgado," he says, pointing to the name stitched onto his white coat. "I'm a doctor." He gives me a second to process that before continuing. "Listen, Allison. You were sedated, but we're bringing you out of the sedation now. You probably feel groggy and confused, but that's completely normal."

I swallow and stop fighting against the restraints. Instead, I look over at one of my bound wrists and then up at the doctor.

"I'll take them off if you promise me you won't pull out your IV line."

I meet his eyes, which are a warm, caramel shade. There's no challenge in the way he holds my gaze, but I can tell he's studying me. Assessing me. Trying to figure out if I'm crazy, just like everyone else here.

"Just give me a nod if we've got a deal," he says.

It's a tough call. I don't want the IV line in my arm. I know why it's there—to run fluids, nutrients, and medicine into my body. To keep me alive and healthy.

Alive and healthy are two things I don't want to be anymore. The flashbacks are merciless, and they never stop, even when I'm asleep. I can't escape my own head as long as I'm alive.

But being tied to this bed is unbearable. The terror I feel at being unable to escape is enough to choke me. I'd agree to anything right now to be freed.

I nod once, and Dr. Delgado leans down to unfasten the first restraint.

"I'm not a fan of restraints," he says as he works. "I think they do more harm than good. But if you're putting yourself in danger, we may not have a choice."

As soon as he gets the first restraint off, he lifts my wrist to examine it. His hand is twice the size of mine, but he has a gentle touch.

There's a little redness from my brief struggle against the restraints, but Dr. Delgado seems to dismiss it. He sets my arm back on the mattress and walks around to the other side of the bed to free my other hand.

"I'm the general practitioner here at Hawthorne," he says. "I'll come see you every day, prescribe meds when you need them, and treat any injuries or illnesses you may get. Dr. Heaton consults with me on her sessions with you, and we collaborate on any prescriptions or treatments for mental health."

He seems more chill than Dr. Tillman, who got aggravated when I wouldn't answer his questions. That son of a bitch threatened to have me sedated several times, and apparently, he went through with it.

"I see we've got a dry-erase board there for you," Dr. Delgado says, nodding at my bedside table. "Anything you want to ask me or tell me?"

I shake my head. The second restraint is removed, and I rub my wrist.

"If you have any problems at all, let me know. You can roam around the place during free hours from 7:00 a.m. to 7:00 p.m."

I look over at the window, where the open curtains reveal a clear blue sky. Most people would call this a beautiful day, but not me. I can't find beauty in a world with such ugliness. A place that would allow the brutal murder of the other half of my heart.

Closing my eyes, I shut out the sunshine. Fuck sunshine. I want dark clouds. Torrential downpours. Destructive tornadoes.

"I've taken you off the sedative, but Allison . . . let me know if you're struggling with anything. Sadness, insomnia . . . whatever it is, I can prescribe you something to help. I'm sure you're still hurting from the loss of your sister. I'm very sorry about that."

My throat tightens and burns. He's the first one to mention her, other than that bitch Dr. Heaton. And I don't like it. It hurts too much to hear anyone speak of her. It brings to the surface what's already horrifyingly real.

I grab the bedcovers, lie down, and curl up, pulling the covers over my head. This doctor seems like a decent enough guy, but I can't listen to him anymore. I need to cry until my head pounds, so I can feel something—anything—other than the ache that's burned its way into my very soul.

Chapter
THREE

"HOW ARE YOU today, Allison?" Dr. Heaton asks, her familiar tone making it seem like we're old friends.

I stare out the window of her office, wondering if the weather outside is as nice as it looks. The sun is shining bright in a clear blue sky again, but it's April. In my hometown of Chicago, April can be a bitch. It's cold, rainy, and dreary.

And I'm even farther north now. I bet it's chilly outside, the sun's rays just giving the illusion of warmth.

"You can talk to me," Heaton says for at least the twentieth time since I've been here. "Everything said in this room is confidential. I'm here to help you work through the grief I know you're feeling."

I glance around her office. There are framed diplomas on the wood-plank walls and bookshelves with books and picture frames arranged just so. The photos show smiling people posing for the camera, all of them smiling so perfectly they could be the paper photos that come in picture frames when you first buy them.

A fountain in the shape of a bunch of bamboo gurgles in a

corner, and neatly trimmed bonsai trees line the ledge of the large window behind Heaton's desk.

Even the box of tissues on the coffee table in front of me has been methodically placed, one corner of the square in front of me so it makes a diamond shape. The top tissue is pulled up, its sides still tucked neatly inside. It looks like a tissue fountain, beautifully shaped into a parallel pattern.

That's not the tissue box of a doctor whose patients feel comfortable crying. If the box were half-empty, with little white specks of tissue dust dotting the coffee table, I'd at least feel like it was okay to use one.

A smile quirks at my lips as I imagine whipping out a tissue or two. I'm picturing Heaton descending on the box right after me to tidy up the tissue fountain and brush away the tissue flecks.

"Why are you smiling, Allison?" The warmth in her tone tells me she thinks it has something to do with her. "Do you see something that made you remember something happy?"

I sigh softly and look at the wall clock. I've got thirty-five minutes left in this hour-long session. I've been at Hawthorne for almost a month, and I never get to go more than two days without coming here for a session.

One of my favorite games to play with myself during our sessions is *"Will she, or won't she?"* Sometimes, Heaton gets so aggravated that she lets me leave early. Other times, she digs in her heels and makes me stay the whole hour. I'm pretty sure she's tried every trick in her shrink bag, from just staring at me in silence for an entire hour, to offering to just cry with me, to jabbing at me in subtle ways designed to get a reaction.

Today is a Monday, so I think she'll keep me the entire hour. She starts her weeks resigned to make me talk.

"We can't make progress this way," she says, crossing one leg over the other in the wingback chair she's sitting in across from me. "I know there are thoughts and feelings happening inside that head of yours, Allison."

I just want to go back to my room and read the book I got from Hawthorne's library. It's the biography of a former prisoner of war, and I'm hooked.

"When I'm concerned about my patients, I take my work home with me." Heaton leans forward in her chair. "And I read through your entire file again over the weekend."

She pauses to let that sink in, like it's going to impress me.

"You and Ava were very close. Twins have a very special bond. You must miss her terribly and feel like you have no one to talk to with her gone."

I turn back to the window and see a big, black bird flying across the expanse of sky. Even if it's cold outside, the breeze in its face has to feel downright glorious.

"The police still haven't made an arrest in Ava's case, you know. If you want to see her killer brought to justice, the best thing you can do is talk to the detectives assigned to the case. They can come here, and I can help you do that. Any detail you recall from that night, no matter how small, may be the lead they've been searching for."

There are more birds visible now, and I watch them flying over the forest in the distance. Do they live nearby, or are they just passing through?

"Okay, Allison," Heaton says, sighing softly. "You can go. Just remember that my door is always open. All progress is good, no matter how slow. You're eating and drinking now, and that's progress we can celebrate."

I give her a tight-lipped half smile and get up from the couch. I'm eating and drinking because it's impossible not to. I can either do it myself, or they'll stick an IV in me.

The CNA assigned to bring me to my session today, Terrance,

is waiting for me in the hallway, smiling at something on his phone.

"Back to your room, Miss Allison?" he asks, putting the phone in his pocket.

Just like every time I leave Heaton's office, I lead the way to the wide stairway, walk up, and make my way to my room. I pour myself a big glass of water from the pitcher beside my bed and then curl up in the chair in the corner of my room with my book, setting my water on the table beside mine.

"You just push your call button if you need anything," Terrance says with a smile.

I meet his eyes in acknowledgment, and he leaves the room. I'm blissfully alone once again.

It's just too hard to be inside my head, and I fear it always will be. I've finally found a way to escape into someone else's head—books.

As soon as I start reading, I feel like the bird I saw outside Heaton's window. Careless and free.

Chapter
FOUR

THE COOL, RAINY April finally gives way to May. It's muddy and there's still a chill in the air some days, but everyone knows the worst of the Montana weather is behind us now.

Hawthorne Hill's stable opened back up for patient use today, and the dining room is buzzing with excitement from those who went riding for the first time since fall.

"You see that new mare?" Leonard asks as he sits down across from me at one of several tables in the dining room.

"Yeah, she's a beauty."

"Bet we'll see some Level Twos workin' up to Level One just so they can ride her." He chuckles and puts his fork into the steaming chicken pot pie on his plate.

I nod in agreement. Hawthorne's patients are classified into three different levels, and only Level Ones get to do outdoor activities.

"Did you ride Thunder today?" I ask him.

"Sure did."

His wide smile says it all. Leonard loves that horse. Other than the stable master, Leonard and I are the only ones who can ride Thunder. He's a massive stallion who's a bully when he wants to be.

"So when are we going camping, Doc? You know I'm first on your list for this season."

"We can go this weekend."

He smiles. "That's what I'm talkin' about." His expression turns cloudy. "Well, unless the phone lines have been tapped. I don't want no government types following us out there, you know?"

"I think we'll be okay."

"You don't know what they're capable of, Doc." His eyes widen with fear. "They're planning something. I know it."

When Leonard starts to go down this path, I try to redirect his attention. Sometimes it works, sometimes it doesn't.

"Are you hanging around for movie night after dinner?" I ask him as I scoop up a bite of chicken pot pie.

"You know it. What about you?"

"Wish I could, but I've got paperwork to catch up on."

Hawthorne sends quarterly summaries about patients to their families, and I have to read and sign off on all of them. I could take them to my cabin, but I might as well just stay here.

As soon as I'm done with dinner, I go into my office and close the door. I've been needing to get to these reports for several days, but I've been too busy. We have a new patient who was sent here after he had a break with reality and went on a shooting rampage. He was found mentally unfit for trial. Since he's a strapping guy with serious mental issues, I haven't wanted to leave him alone with any of the staff. A patient like him requires extra security.

Some of the reports I read detail small victories. A patient who obsessively pulled out her own hair has cut back on the habit after taking up drawing. Another admitted he'd sent threatening letters to women, which he'd been denying for the entire year he's been here.

I don't see much backsliding this quarter, which is good. But a strong majority of the patients remain the same as they've been every quarter I've read and signed off on these reports. Many of them are getting treatment that improves their quality of life, and I like being part of that.

Some people are broken, but not many. I find that nearly everyone thrives when we focus on their strengths instead of their weaknesses.

The final report in my pile is the shortest. Allison Cole has made progress. She's eating and drinking now and spends her days reading in her room. Sometimes her nights, too. Dr. Heaton is critical of letting Allison escape into books instead of "helping" her confront reality.

But I tell Heaton in every weekly staff meeting that help is a two-way street. Until Allison is ready to face what happened, we can't make her do it. And we shouldn't.

We still don't know if she's even physically able to talk. Her vocal cords may have been damaged by the strangulation. It would help if she'd use the dry-erase board to tell us things, but she doesn't want to.

Pain affects us in unique ways. I bury mine deep and seek outlets for it. Drinking was the worst of those outlets. Now I use work to avoid confronting past mistakes and the fallout I caused.

It's eight thirty at night when I finish the reports and get up from my desk. As soon as I open the door to my office, I hear muffled laughter from the movie room and smile. We usually play light comedies on movie nights, because dramas upset some patients.

I skipped dessert after dinner, but the smell of Black Forest cake still lingers in the air, so I head to the kitchen to swipe a piece. As I'm grabbing a plastic-wrapped saucer, I think of Allison again and reach for another one, then get two forks.

There's a back staircase to the second floor, and I find total silence when I walk up there. Allison's room is near the end of the hall, and when I get there, I knock on her half-open door and look inside.

"Hey, you still awake?" I ask.

She looks over from the chair in the corner, where she's curled up with a book, the lamp on the table next to her casting a soft glow.

"Thought you might like some of this," I say, walking into the room and setting a saucer on the table. "Mind if I sit?"

Her lips turn up just a touch, and she looks at the end of her bed. I sit down there and peel the plastic wrap back from my cake, taking a bite.

"Can I ask what you're reading?"

She looks up, holding my gaze for a couple seconds before lifting the book from her lap to show me the title.

"*Anna Karenina.*" I nod. "Good choice."

Allison passed her first thirty days here with good behavior, so she no longer has to wear the blue scrubs of a Level Two patient. She's a Level One now, but the only perk she seems to be taking advantage of is wearing her own clothes. Tonight, she's wearing gray sweat pants cut off just above the knee and a Chicago Bears T-shirt that looks soft and well-worn.

"I read that in a college lit class." I finished my cake in three big bites, so I set my plate next to me on the bed. "I was in a fraternity, and I skipped a party we were hosting on a Friday night to read *Anna Karenina*. Went to the library instead. Never heard the end of it. Usually, I was up for a party every Friday night, but there was something about that book . . . I had to know what happened, you know?"

She smiles in answer.

"It's probably how you feel right now, but I'm here keeping you from it."

Her smile widens and she meets my eyes. It's the first time

I've seen a true spark of happiness in her.

"So you like classics." I think back to my college lit class. "Have you read *Tarzan?*"

The shake of her head is almost imperceptible. I feel a surge of satisfaction, but I hold it in. This is the only time Allison has communicated with anyone from Hawthorne in any conscious way. I can tell she's unhappy when she narrows her eyes and when she's overwhelmed because she stares out the window, but that's not communication.

"It's a great story. More than just a Disney movie," I say. "Not that the movie wasn't good. And the soundtrack's pretty great, too."

I get up from my seat on her bed and pick up my plate. "So we both like classic literature, but maybe the Black Forest cake is just my thing." I reach for the plate on the table next to her, arching my brows in question.

She reaches out and puts her fingertips on my wrist, gently pushing it away from the plate of cake.

"We agree on the cake, too, then. I think I'm gonna go grab another piece before I head home, actually." I walk toward the hall-way, turning to face her when I'm in the doorway. "Night, Allison."

She meets my eyes again, and I get a slight nod. The whole way back to the kitchen, I can't keep the grin from my face, because another small victory just happened.

Chapter
FIVE

EATING THE CAKE means I have to brush my teeth again, but it's worth it. After that, I turn out the lights in my room, get in bed, and switch on my small reading lamp to get in some more *Anna Karenina*.

That interaction with Dr. Delgado almost felt like a conversation. It was nice. I've gotten used to people not even talking to me here because they know they'll be met with silence.

The CNA doing night checks just smiles when she peeks inside my room and sees me reading. Before I came here, my pre-bedtime ritual was scrolling through my phone, which I no longer have and no longer care about. I never used to read books. Now they're my lifeline.

I make it until almost eleven, and then my eyelids get too heavy to continue reading. After sliding my book onto the nightstand, I switch off my reading light and let sleep take over.

A deep voice sounds inside my head.

"Who killed your sister, Allison? You know who it was, don't you? Tell me. Tell me."

I try to reach into the darkness, but my hands won't move. A sound rumbles in my throat against my will.

"Tell me who killed your sister." The voice is closer now, more insistent.

In my dreams, I still talk. I scream and cry and let out everything that haunts me. Though I can't even understand what I'm saying, I know that's what I'm doing now.

"You saw her die," the voice says. "You know what happened. Don't you want the killer to be caught? Only you hold the key, Allison. Tell me who killed your sister."

I try to push the voice away, but I'm weighted down, trapped in a fog I can't even see through. The fog only gets cloudier, and soon I stop trying to find my way out of it. The voice is gone now, and I don't want to find it again.

THE NEXT DAY, my breakfast tray has the same three things I order every morning: a small dish of oatmeal, a piece of wheat toast, and a cup of coffee. It's like room service at a nice hotel, except the dishes are plastic and I don't have to tip the person who brings it.

I sit in my corner chair to eat, reading my book as I nibble on the food and down the coffee. When I shift in my seat, movement outside the window of my room catches my attention.

There's a man riding a beautiful black horse across a field. He's leaning down, a hand on the horse's neck. The look on his face is pure elation, his smile warming my heart.

Other than my trips down to Dr. Heaton's office, I don't leave my room. But something about the scene outside my window makes me want to. I've been here for more than six weeks, but I still don't know much about this place.

I put my book down and dress in dark jeans and a gray T-shirt with three-quarter sleeves, then slide into black ballet flats from my closet. The Hawthorne people did a good job buying me clothes

I feel comfortable wearing.

When I venture out of my room and walk down the wide, open staircase, no one seems to notice me. There are a few people drawing and coloring at a small round table in the great room.

"Good to see you, Allison," a woman in the gray scrubs of a Hawthorne CNA says.

Another woman looks up at me from her spot on a leather sofa.

"Hey! You're out of your room." She gets up and walks over to me. "Can I just tell you how glad I am to see you? You're the only woman in here who's remotely close to my age. I mean, other than Clara McMahon, but she's a sociopath on Level Three." She rolls her eyes. "Can't exactly hang out with a sociopath, you know what I mean?"

She looks like a teenager, her face fresh and her blond hair in a loose braid. She's lithe and not much over five feet tall.

"I'm Morgan Tyler," she says, holding out her hand.

I'm a little baffled, but I don't want to be rude, so I shake it. She grins at me.

"And you're Allison. I know you don't talk, or can't, and it's totally cool. I mean, I talk enough for both of us." Another grin. "You're wondering how old I am, aren't you? I'm eighteen." She points past the huge stone fireplace. "I'm gonna snag another one of those blueberry muffins from breakfast. Want to come with me? I can give you the lowdown on this place."

Might as well. I'm not doing anything else. I follow Morgan past the fireplace, and she takes my arm like we're old friends.

"I'm not crazy, by the way. You're probably wondering why I'm here if I'm not crazy. I mean, it's not a secret or anything. No one's story is secret here. When I was fifteen, my stepdad raped me. He married my mom for her money and told me we'd be getting to know each other real well. He was a big hunter, you know? So when he was asleep, I took one of his shotguns and blew his dick off."

My mouth falls open in shock. Did she just say she . . .

"Yeah. I shot him right in the dick. Wasn't trying to kill him, but I did. Not much of a loss to the world, though. Anyway, I was charged as an adult, but my mom hired a fancy attorney who got me a deal where I get to be here instead of prison. Temporary insanity, I think they called it."

Morgan pushes open a set of double doors, and we walk into a huge kitchen with wood-plank floors, marble counters, and wide stainless-steel appliances.

"I work here," she says, opening a container on the counter and taking out a blueberry muffin with streusel on top. "Want one?"

I shake my head slightly.

She takes a small bite of the muffin and leads the way out of the kitchen.

"Level Ones can have jobs here," she says. "We also get to wear regular clothes instead of scrubs, and we can do outside stuff like horseback riding and fishing. Dr. D takes Level Ones camping on weekends. We can have computers, but no Internet, so what's the point?"

She stops in front of a set of glass double doors. "You want to go outside?"

I shrug and she pushes the doors open. The air is cool and smells lightly of grass. I haven't felt the sun on my skin in a long time, and I soak it in.

We sit down on a wood bench, and Morgan resumes talking. "You can get a room on the first level if you ask. All the Level Ones can. Level Twos wear blue scrubs, like you had on when you first got here. Most of them are functionally mentally ill. They're not gonna hurt themselves or anyone else, you know? Paranoia, anxiety, that kind of thing. Crazytown is on Level Three. Those are your psychopaths, schizophrenics, OCDs . . . there are even a couple murderers up there."

My alarm must register on my face because she laughs and says, "Don't worry. The security is tight up there. It takes a retinal scan and a password to open the doors."

I take a deep breath as it hits me that though this place looks like a high-end lodge, it's a mental hospital. It's a beautiful one, but the patients have the same illnesses and challenges as those at any other facility. I have to watch my back.

Though I've been looking out the window of my room for nearly fifty days now, the view is still breathtaking. I think it's because now I'm not just looking, but also feeling the spring air on my cheeks and hearing the sway of the grass and the songs of the birds.

Hawthorne Hill overlooks a huge, open field that spans all the way around one side of the lodge. That side is where the stables are. People are riding horses in and out of a fenced pasture there. The other side of the lodge has several cabins spread out near the edge of a forest.

Past the open field, there's a mountain range. It's spectacular and unlike anything I've ever seen.

"You should come down for dinner tonight," Morgan says. "I'll save you a seat. I don't work in the kitchen at dinnertime."

I nod, and she lights up with happiness.

"Hey, can I ask you something? *Can* you talk?" She lowers her brows conspiratorially. "You could like . . . raise your hand if you can. We could come up with a code that only we understand."

I just smile. I can't help liking Morgan, but I'm not looking to become an eighteen-year-old girl's BFF.

"Maybe later," she says, shrugging. "At least you're coming to dinner tonight." She looks over at the stables and then turns back to me. "Also, the room next to mine is open. On the first floor. I'm just saying."

A CNA walks out the double doors we came out of. "There

you are, Morgan. You coming down to the stables to go riding?"

"Oh, yeah." She gets up and gestures for me to follow. "Come on, Allison. You can ride, too."

I shake my head. She shrugs and follows the CNA to the stone path that leads down the hill to the stables.

Curiosity leads me to walk around to the side of the lodge where the cabins are. The log homes are built in the same style as the lodge, but on a miniature scale. Each one has a small front porch with a rocking chair on it. The row of cabins stretches back far—there are at least twenty of them. This must be where Hawthorne's staffers live.

I keep walking around the lodge, and in the back, I see a log shed and another, larger log home. There's a huge deck and a stone patio with lawn furniture and a grill. Tall trees shade everything.

On my way to the patio, I pass a small patch of freshly sown dirt. It looks like someone's tiny garden, with neat rows ready to be seeded.

And then I see my personal paradise—a rope hammock hanging between two trees. It's a perfect spot to read. I can picture myself spending all afternoon right there, the breeze blowing through my hair as I'm cocooned in the hammock.

I walk back into the main building through a set of open double doors on the deck and then make my way up to my room. When I go to pick up the *Anna Karenina* hardback from the nightstand, I'm stopped by the sight of something on my bed.

As soon as I get close enough to see what it is, I smile and pick it up. It's a paperback of *Tarzan*. When I open it up, I see the name *Daniel Delgado* scrawled on the inside cover.

I take both books to the hammock. Looks like I found my next read.

Chapter
SIX

BRODY TILLMAN IS straight up terrified of our new patient. I knew it from the moment he asked two male CNAs to restrain Chad Larimore before we even walked into his room.

I told the CNAs to hold off and wait outside the door. Brody arched his brows, mumbled, "It's your funeral" and then walked in a good four feet behind me.

"Morning, Chad," I say in a neutral tone.

His low laugh and the wild look in his eyes are meant to intimidate me, but I walk up to his bedside.

"Those nurses sent you in here 'cause they're scared I'm gonna hurt 'em," he says, sounding satisfied.

"I already warned you once, and I'm told you threatened to rape the nurse who came to see you this morning."

"It's *so good* when they fight me." He grabs his dick beneath the bedsheet and starts stroking himself.

"From now on, Dr. Tillman and I will see to your medical needs." I step aside so Chad can see Tillman.

"Well, aren't you cute?" Chad says to Tillman. "Come say hi,

I don't bite hard."

Tillman's feet are rooted to the floor. Chad laughs again, still jerking off under the covers.

"Only male CNAs will assist you," I continue. "You can't threaten our staff, Chad."

"You'll be sedated and restrained the next time it happens." Tillman's effort at sounding tough falls short.

"Restrained? Sounds kinky," Chad says, his tone gleeful.

Like all of Level Three, Chad's room is bare bones. The staff at Hawthorne has learned over the years that psychotic and suicidal patients can make use of unexpected things to hurt themselves or others. Chad only has a bed and a Styrofoam pitcher of water on the floor. All the windows at Hawthorne are made of extra-thick, shatterproof glass, but on Level Three, the blinds were installed between two panes of thick glass, and they're opened and closed from outside the room.

Chad has very little stimulus, but he's rejected every opportunity to fix that, shredding the pages of a book and eating it a couple days ago.

"You won't wear me out, Chad," I say, holding his gaze. "I was in the army for a few years, and after that, I went into emergency medicine. I've dealt with all kinds of people."

"People who skin others for fun?" He quickly jumps to his knees on the mattress, his wiry frame on full display since he refuses to wear his gown.

I shrug. "Probably. I was stationed in Afghanistan for a while, and there were some sick fuckers over there."

He steps out of bed and stalks toward Tillman. Tillman shifts his eyes to me and then back to Chad.

"You think I only like to fuck unwilling women?" His laugh is more like a maniacal shriek.

Tillman puts his hands out in front of him.

"Get your ass back to the bed, Chad," I say.

"Not yet." He moves closer to Tillman, who looks disgusted and scared at the same time.

Tillman needs to assert himself, but he's clearly not going to. I approach them, and Chad stops moving.

"You'd be scared of me if you weren't so big," he says to me. "You think your size keeps you safe from me, but you're wrong."

"Take your best shot, then."

He stares at me for a couple seconds before saying, "Not now."

"Not ever. You'll learn that life is better here when you co-operate."

Chad grabs his dick and starts jerking off again. How the guy can get hard right now, while arguing with me, I have no idea. He really does have deep psychological problems. His file was one of the most disturbing I've ever read.

"I hear there's a hot mute woman in the house," he says. "I would *love* to get my hands on her."

I stiffen. The thought of him even being in the same room with Allison makes me sick. And who the fuck is telling Chad about our other patients? I'm laying down a new rule at the next staff meeting. Not that I should even need to.

"You're in an isolation wing," I say, forcing neutrality I don't feel into my tone. "So that's not happening."

"Mute," he muses. "I would miss the screaming an awful lot. But then . . . the things I could do without anyone knowing if I could just get her alone."

He laughs gleefully, and a muscle in my jaw twitches. I could wipe that smile off his face so easily, but I can't let my feelings show. I remind myself that he'll never even *see* Allison, let alone get his hands on her.

"We'll leave you to it," I say. "Terrance will be delivering your meal trays today, and Dr. Tillman will check on you tomorrow."

Tillman hightails it for the door, probably not wanting to turn his back on Chad without my cover. The door buzzes as it locks behind us, and I point to a small conference room down the hall.

"Let's go," I say to Tillman.

As soon as we're inside and the door is closed, he lets out a deep exhale. "Man, that guy is fucking *off*."

"You do realize you work at a mental hospital?"

"Yeah, but . . . he's missing something. There's no remorse."

"That's often the case with psychopaths."

He sits down in a chair on the other side of the small conference table, but I just stand behind one, holding on to the top of it.

"Psychopaths can also be charming and are often intelligent," I continue.

"What's with the lesson? I know all this." Tillman glares at me.

"Do you? Because you just gave him the upper hand in there. He knows you're scared of him, and he'll play on that."

Tillman scoffs. "I wasn't scared."

"Don't bullshit me. It's Saturday, and I was supposed to leave for a hike with patients ten minutes ago."

"The guy's a *murderer*, Daniel."

"Yeah, but he's not gonna murder you with a bed. Bring Terrance in there with you if you need to, but don't let Chad control the dynamic of your interactions with him. If it gets out of control, you leave. But don't ever leave with your tail between your legs."

"He needs to be sedated and restrained, man. That guy is dangerous."

My muscles tense as I take a deep breath and look down at the floor, trying to keep my cool.

"Everyone here is potentially dangerous, Brody. Either to themselves or others. Anyone with a mental illness that requires inpatient treatment needs to be treated with respect and compassion, but also with no doubt about who's in charge."

"You." There's an edge of bitterness in his tone.

"When it's you and a patient, *you're* in charge."

"Until you correct me later."

I shake my head and glare at him. "Always in private. Hawthorne has a philosophy about patient care. It's my job to see that we all stay on the same page about it."

His nod is reluctant. "It just seems like it's *your* philosophy."

"Yeah, I happen to agree with Hawthorne's approach to patient care. Why do you think I'm here?"

"I figured it was because you couldn't get hired anywhere else after your license was suspended."

The air changes in the room, turning thick with tension. I let Tillman's words hang in the air for a few seconds before responding.

"So you looked up my licensing records."

He gives me a smug look. "Is the Hawthorne administration aware you lost your license?"

"Yes. They are aware my license was suspended. I was in good standing when I came here."

I can see the disappointment on his face. He was probably saving that information and planning to deliver a knockout punch with it, but it was more like a weak slap.

"My job here is secure, Tillman. And yours will be, too, if you'll take my constructive criticism and learn from it. I'm talking to you now because I don't want shit to go bad. The sooner you assert yourself with a patient like Chad, the less likely he is to try anything with you. And if you're not comfortable treating him, let me know and I'll do it."

"No, I'm fine."

I nod. "Okay. I have to go."

I don't wait for him to leave the conference room with me. Instead, I wave at the nurse sitting at the Level Three station, and she buzzes me through the door to the elevator. There, I bend down for the retinal scanner and enter my code into a keypad.

I'm pissed at Tillman. Guys like him just love being assholes. There are days I think it would be less trouble to handle all work myself than to constantly have to oversee and correct him.

The elevator takes me down to the first floor, and as soon as the doors open, a small group of patients standing in the great room turns toward me.

"There's Dr. D," Leonard says.

Three patients are gathered for a morning hike. We only have seven Level One patients right now, and the others must be doing something else.

Leonard is standing with Morgan and Tim, all three of them wearing pants, sweatshirts, and hiking boots.

"Be right there," I say to them. "I need to grab my backpack from my office."

I jog down the hallway and walk through my open office doorway. Two books on the outer corner of the desk catch my attention. I pick up the top one, which is my old copy of *Tarzan* that I left for Allison.

When I open the cover, there's a small, cream-colored piece of paper with neat handwriting.

I had no idea this story was so romantic. Other than the end, that is. Jane should have chosen Tarzan. But other than my broken heart, I loved it.

After setting the note back inside the cover, I close the book and return it to my bookshelf. I feel a strong urge to write a note back to her. If that's how she wants to communicate with me, I'll take it. But I don't want to push my luck.

I pick up the other book from my desk. She left a hardback of *Pride and Prejudice* from Hawthorne Hill's library beneath *Tarzan*.

Looks like it's my turn to read a book she recommends. I tuck the book into the worn leather messenger bag I carry between my home and office every day and then pick up my backpack from behind my desk.

It has first aid supplies, my utility knife, climbing ropes, water, and a few other emergency supplies. I have to be prepared for anything when I take patients into the woods.

I head back to the great room and tell the hikers we're heading out. We're on our way out the door when I see someone running down the open stairway out the corner of my eye.

"Hey, you made it!" Morgan says with a squeal.

It's Allison, dressed in jeans and a thin black hoodie. She's wearing a Cubs baseball hat, her dark ponytail pulled through the hole in the back of it.

When she looks at me, there's a question in her eyes. Her cheeks are flushed pink from the run down the stairs, and I find myself just looking at her for a couple seconds.

I've never seen a patient as anything but a patient, but right now, I'm just looking at a pretty woman. A *very* pretty woman.

"Um . . . you want to join us?" I finally manage.

Her lips curve up slightly into a smile.

"Let's go," Tim says from behind me. "We were supposed to leave eighteen minutes ago."

He's a middle-aged guy with OCD, but with the help of a strict routine, he's pretty functional.

"Sorry about that, Tim," I say. "Let's go, guys."

Leonard leads us down the stone path that takes us to the staff cabins, and then another hundred yards to the edge of the woods.

"Everyone has to stay together," I remind them. "And there's nothing but woods for a hundred miles, so don't try to run. I'll catch you if you do, and you'll get bumped back to Level Two."

I tell Leonard to keep leading so I can stay in the middle of the group. Tim's behind him, and Morgan and Allison are behind me. Morgan's talking up a storm, as usual. Sometimes I wish she'd take a breath once in a while, but I can't help liking her. Any teenage girl who would shoot her piece of shit stepfather in the junk has guts, and I admire that.

The forest cover quickly becomes dense, and the terrain gets a little less even. I've done this walk dozens of times now, and I know intuitively where the path starts to get rocky.

I thought I understood mental illness before I came to Hawthorne, but I only knew it in a clinical sense. At this luxurious lodge in the middle of nowhere, I've seen patients thrive with an approach that combines traditional medicine with the outdoors. Hiking is therapeutic for many of them. Hell, it's therapeutic for me. Out here, there's no pressure or worry. This forest reminds me that inner peace is possible. I've had to hike and climb for days or weeks on end to find that peace sometimes, but it's always waiting for me.

"I've missed the sound of that creek," Leonard says from the front of the line.

The sound of rippling water starts faintly but grows stronger as we get closer. Finally, I can hear it over Morgan's chatter about eye makeup.

"Cross the rocks, Doc?" Leonard calls back to me.

"Yep. Be careful."

The creek is about ten feet wide here, and we cross it by stepping on a series of large rocks I put in the water. I'm planning to build a bridge over the creek this summer, but for now, the rocks are the only way to keep our boots dry.

Leonard is spry for his age, and he hops from rock to rock easily. Tim goes slower, counting each rock as he steps on it.

My legs are so long that the crossing is easy for me. When I get to the other side, I set my backpack on the ground. Morgan has a skeptical expression as she looks at me. She's done this hike many times, but the water is higher than usual today.

"Easy does it," I say. "Just go slowly. Put your arms out for balance if you need to."

She takes a deep breath and practically runs across the rocks, her toes barely touching them. Damn. To be eighteen years old again.

"Your turn," she says to Allison.

Allison goes slowly, putting her arms out and stepping on each rock with both feet before moving on. The final leap is the biggest, and her eyes meet mine right before she sets off.

I can see she's going to fall a little short and land in the water, so I grab her in midair and set her feet on the ground. My big hands span almost her entire waist, and I leave them there for a beat longer than needed.

The warm shine in her soft brown eyes is better than a spoken thank you. Leonard is pointing something out to Tim and Morgan, so Allison and I have a moment of silent but palpable energy between us.

I clear my throat and turn to the others, checking myself. I can't be attracted to a patient, and I sure as hell can't do anything to make it look like I am in front of *other* patients. For a few seconds there, I lost myself.

"I'll lead from here," I say to Leonard.

"You got it, Doc," he says, falling in behind me.

For the rest of the hike, I don't even make eye contact with Allison. Whatever happened between us at the creek, I can't let it happen again. There's too much on the line for me to risk crossing any professional line with a patient. Even one as beautiful and enigmatic as Allison.

Chapter
SEVEN

THE GRASS GETS greener and flowers start blooming as May comes to a close and June begins. I find a new normal at Hawthorne, spending my days walking, reading, and horseback riding.

The outdoors was never my thing before. I spent nearly all my time in downtown Chicago. I've gotten accustomed to the sweet smell of hay in the horse stable and the fragrance of pine in the woods here. I didn't realize before that the only things I ever smelled outside were car exhaust and the occasional hot dog stand.

It's quiet here. When flashbacks overwhelm me, I can always find a secluded spot to work through it on my own. The flashbacks are always worse on the nights I have the dream. It's always the same—that voice probing me about what I know while I fight to resist it.

Though I didn't think I'd ever find a life I wanted to live again, I slowly am. I spend time with Morgan every day, and I even signed up to go on a camping trip with Daniel this weekend. I like being around him. We've been exchanging books back and forth for several weeks now. A few days after our first hiking trip, he returned

Pride and Prejudice to me with a note tucked into the front cover.

> *Enjoyed this very much. A woman who's perceptive, whip-smart, funny, and able to admit when she's wrong? I think I'm in love.*
>
> *Try this one next.*
>
> *Daniel*

It was *Treasure Island*, which I loved. There's something about reading the books he recommends that makes me feel like I know him. Since I don't need medical care, I don't see him much in person. He keeps pretty busy tending to the Level Twos and Threes.

But Dr. Heaton, I see with annoying regularity. Every Monday, Wednesday, and Friday I have to endure an hour in her office. She's devoted, I'll give her that. Sometimes I feel like her life mission is to hear my voice. It grates on me, though, that she thinks I need to spill my guts and have some cathartic moment with her to feel whole again.

I'll never feel whole again. I've accepted that, and I've found people like Morgan and Daniel who seem to like me as I am.

I'm walking to Dr. Heaton's small waiting room for a Wednesday appointment now, my mind still on my horseback ride this morning. I've been riding a mare named Pearl, and I've gotten attached to her. Her ears perk up and her tail swishes when she sees me, probably because I usually bring an apple for her.

I'm about to open the door to Dr. Heaton's waiting room when someone opens it from the inside. It's Daniel, wearing a pale blue polo, jeans, and his trademark hiking books. He has them in brown and gray, and today he's wearing the brown ones.

"Hey, Allison," he says, closing the door behind him.

A smile creeps onto my lips, and I feel my cheeks getting the slightest bit warm. I can't help it—there's something about being in Daniel's presence that always makes me happy. He's not what I'd expect from a doctor. It's not just the jeans and hiking boots, but also the tattoos I can see on his arms when he wears short sleeves and doesn't have his white doctor coat on. He usually has a five o'clock shadow, and his dark hair is overdue for a trim. Everything about him is casual.

He gestures toward the book I have tucked under my arm. It's *Lord of the Rings*, the latest book he loaned me.

"Hope you're liking it," he says.

I nod and meet his eyes for a couple seconds before reaching for the door to Dr. Heaton's office. He beats me to it, opening the door for me.

"See you around," he says.

I hope so. Morgan said a nurse named Sara has the hots for him, and when she speculated about whether they were sleeping together, I was disappointed by the thought of him having a girlfriend.

"Come on in, Allison," Dr. Heaton says as soon as I walk into her waiting room. "I was just looking for you."

She's wearing a navy pantsuit with nude heels, looking more ready for a meeting about a corporate merger than a counseling session. And her office is spotless as usual, everything in its perfect place. She has a new small glass sculpture on her end table in the shape of a teardrop.

I sit down in my usual spot on her leather couch, the tinkle of her bamboo fountain already on my nerves. The creeks we cross in the woods on our hikes have a soothing, melodic sound. The fountain is supposed to mimic it, but it's just a knock-off. I prefer the real thing.

"So," she says, closing her office door. "Is there anything you'd like to talk about?"

I shake my head, and she sits down in her chair across from

the couch, crossing her legs.

"Allison, I spoke to a detective at the Chicago PD this morning. It's been ninety days since Ava's murder, and they still don't have any leads. It's their policy to move cases to their Cold Case section at that point until a lead surfaces."

I set *Lord of the Rings* next to me on the couch, and I lay my palm over its cover as she speaks, keeping my expression neutral.

"I've done some more research on your background, and I talked to the detective for a while earlier, hoping to come up with something I've missed. I can't overlook facts, though. And it's a fact that while you *may* be physically unable to talk, you can still write." She leans forward in her chair, her eyes locked on me. "Yet you choose to say nothing about that night. You, the *only* witness. The only one who could tell the police what the murderer looks like."

I turn my face toward the window, searching for the birds I like to watch during these sessions. With something else to focus on, I can tune Dr. Heaton out.

She sits back in her chair, her crossed hands sitting primly in her lap. "Ava was always the more popular one. Not just a cheerleader, but also an award-winning member of the high school debate team. You were always on the sidelines. Your father died when the two of you were three, and you were raised by a single mother whose fashion line took off and made millions. You both studied business in college, but you became a yoga instructor after graduation and Ava started a line of handbags that launched her career as a highly successful fashion designer. You were single, and she was engaged to Dax Caldwell, a millionaire entrepreneur himself."

Finally, a bird flies into view. Its wings spread, it looks like a savior, swooping in to save me from Dr. Heaton's latest attempt at making me talk.

"She had it all, Allison, and once again, you were on the side-lines. I can see how that would make you . . . jealous. And it's starting to make sense to me now. Why you don't want the police to solve your sister's murder. I think you know exactly who did it."

I'm breathing harder, clutching the spine of the book and wishing I could be anywhere but here. I'd finally found some emotional distance, and I've been plunged right back into the darkness I never thought I'd escape from.

"Maybe things took a bad turn," she continues. "Maybe you just wanted to scare her. It could have been a robbery gone wrong. Or maybe it went exactly as you planned. I can't see this any other way, Allison. You know details about that night that could lead to an arrest, and you won't share them. You don't want this case to be solved. All you care about—"

Her words are clawing at my neck, making it impossible to breathe. I stand up, grab the teardrop sculpture from her table, and launch it toward the wall. It shatters, and the shards fall to the floor.

My chest is heaving in and out, and I squeeze my eyes closed. Dr. Heaton must have pushed a button I can't see, because a security guard comes flying through the door at me.

"On the ground!" he yells, reaching for something at his waist.

I just look at him, suddenly weary. It's Jeff, and he knows who I am. He knows I'm not armed. But as he advances, eyes narrowed, I realize I'll probably be considered unpredictable and off-balance now, just like so many other patients here.

I lay down on my stomach and hear more footsteps coming into the room. A needle is poked into my arm, and I squeeze my eyes shut, tears dropping onto the carpet of Dr. Heaton's office.

Was it Daniel who sedated me? Does he think I planned my sister's murder, too? Does he think I'm mentally unstable? He probably won't send me books or write me notes anymore.

The voices around me become softer, and my worries start to slide away as I lose consciousness.

I FEEL GROGGY when I open my eyes and see that I'm in my room. It's still daytime, and I can't figure out why I'm here. When I try to sit up, I'm too weak. My head falls back against the pillow.

There's movement in the chair in the corner of the room.

"Hey, Allison, it's me. Daniel." He stands up from the chair and sets a book down on the table.

He's wearing dark reading glasses. His pale blue polo reminds me of seeing him in the hallway earlier, and then it hits me all at once. I'm in bed because I was sedated in Dr. Heaton's office.

"You're safe," he says as he approaches the side of the bed.

I trust Daniel. He's never given me any reason to doubt him. As I look up at him, my racing pulse slowly starts to calm.

"Want me to help you sit up?" he asks me.

I nod. He leans down to help me and I smell his warm, woodsy scent. Gently, he puts his hands under my arms and helps me slide up into a sitting position. I'm still feeling a little loopy, though, and I lean my head back against the pillow he moves for me.

He walks to the other side of the bed, where there's a pitcher of water and a cup, and pours me a cup of water. I drink it all.

"I wish I could hear what happened from you," he says as I hand the cup back to him. "I know it's unlike you to lash out for no reason."

What did Dr. Heaton tell him? I close my eyes, imagining the worst.

He pulls the chair up to the side of the bed and sits down. I look over at him.

"I'll always be straight with you, Allison. Because of the property damage, we have to move you back to Level Two. But with thirty days of no issues, you'll be back at Level One. And I want to apologize for the nurse's sedation of you. I'm sure it wasn't necessary, and I've had a talk with the staff involved in it. Sedation is supposed to be the last option here, not the first."

I nod and sigh softly.

Daniel is leaning forward in his chair, his legs spread and his elbows on his knees. He's so big he takes up every inch of the chair I can curl up in. After a few seconds of silence, he reaches toward my bed. I think he may take my hand, and my heart leaps at the thought, but he stops short and just sets his hand on the mattress next to me.

"I don't want to force you to talk to me, Allison. But I want you to know that if something's not right here, you can trust me with it. I've got this gut feeling that you didn't lose your shit for no reason in Heaton's office. You can write me a note if you ever need to tell me something, and it'll stay between us."

I look over at my nightstand, where the dry-erase board is sitting. The housekeeper dusts it off when she cleans because I've never touched it.

Daniel understands. He picks it up and gives it to me, also passing me the black marker.

I uncap the marker and write.

I don't want to see Dr. Heaton anymore.

He nods. "Okay. You don't have to. Is there something I need to know about her?"

I shake my head. I don't want him to know what she said. Below the first message, I write another one.

Do you think I'm crazy?

"No."

Do you say that about everyone here? Do you think some of the people here are crazy?

His lips curve up into a smile.

"I don't use the word crazy. Some people here are mentally ill. I think whatever you're dealing with is probably situational."

I lean over to the nightstand and grab a tissue, wiping off the messages on the board so I can write another one.

Will you still bring me books?

"Yeah, absolutely."

Sara, the nurse Morgan says is hot for Daniel, looks into my room.

"Dr. D, you're late for the staff meeting."

"I'll be right there," he says.

I write out another message.

What should I call you? Dr. Delgado? Dr. D? Dr. Lumberjack?

The smile returns and he shakes his head.

"Call me Daniel." He stands up, towering over me. "I wish I could stay, but I've got to go. Are you good?"

I nod and wipe the board clean.

"Okay. I'll reschedule your camping trip for the first weekend after your thirty days are up."

He picks up the book from the table, holding it up so I can see that it's *The Scarlet Letter*, which I left in his office Friday. That makes me smile.

When he walks out, I return the dry-erase board to the table and pour some more water, drinking it all.

It's back to blue patient scrubs for me. And I can't ride Pearl or hike for a month. It hits me harder than I thought it would. I curl up under the covers of the bed, feeling unable to face anyone. I'll be the talk of Hawthorne Hill for a day or two. Anytime someone gets moved back a level, it's gossip fodder.

I don't want to spend a month as a Level Two, and I'll miss being outside every day. But the worst part of all this is that Dr. Heaton finally won. After more than two months of trying to get to me, she succeeded. At least I won't have to see the smug look of satisfaction on her face.

Chapter
EIGHT

I'M THE LAST one to walk into the staff meeting, and I hear talk about what went down in Dr. Heaton's office earlier with Allison. I still have the image in my mind of her vulnerable expression as she waited for me to tell her if I think she's crazy, and it bothers me to hear her gossiped about. I care about Allison, more than I probably should.

The executive administrator at Hawthorne is Joanne Hawthorne, one of founder Henry Hawthorne's granddaughters. She's focused on reading something on her tablet, but as soon as I walk in and take my seat, she calls the meeting to order.

"Sorry I'm late," I say.

"No apology needed, Dr. Delgado." She peers at me over the top of her glasses. "Patient care comes first."

Only department heads are included in the staff meeting, so the group is small. Besides Dr. Heaton and me, only the heads of nursing, patient recreation, and security are here.

"Allison Cole is a Level Two effective today," Joanne says. "And I've arranged for hospice to come in for James McCord."

James has been at Hawthorne most of his adult life, and the people here are the only family he has. He's never been able to move down to Level One because his behavior is too unpredictable. At age eighty-three, we'll be losing him to congestive heart failure soon.

"He's comfortable," I say.

Joanne moves on to a discussion of security upgrades for Level Three. I'm still thinking about my conversation with Allison, and I look at Heaton. She won't even glance up at me, instead keeping her attention on her tablet.

The meeting is almost an hour long, and Heaton refuses to make eye contact with me through the entire thing. I can't shake the feeling that something prompted Allison to lose her cool with Heaton.

"Dr. Heaton, can you stay?" I ask her when everyone starts to leave the room.

She sits back down, and when it's just the two of us and the door is closed, I say, "What happened with Allison?"

"I already told you, she broke a gift I was given by a former student."

"What happened before that?"

"I was updating her on the police investigation into her sister's death."

I rub the shadow of a beard on my jawline, considering. "Was that really necessary? I'm guessing whatever you said upset her."

Heaton gives me a tight smile. "Psychiatric treatment of the patients here falls under my purview, Dr. Delgado."

"With my oversight."

"With your *general* oversight. I'm certainly not required to get your approval for how I approach sessions with patients."

I exhale heavily, not interested in a debate. "So what was the update? Has someone been arrested?"

"To the contrary, Ava Cole's case is now considered cold." She gives me a knowing look. "Because the only person who can tell the police what happened refuses to."

"Allison may not even remember. She could be suffering from PTSD. It's your job to support her."

"She's not making any progress, Daniel."

I shake my head. "First of all, I disagree. And since when do we require progress?"

"Progress is always my goal. Why spin my wheels if I can help someone?"

"Do you think you helped Allison today?"

Heaton leans forward, her eyes narrowed. "It's not your job to question my methods. I was recruited to come here for my expertise, so don't treat me like I'm your intern. Save your superiority complex for Brody Tillman."

"I'll question your methods when something like this happens. I've never seen the slightest sign of aggression from Allison."

"You do realize she was likely involved in her sister's murder, right?"

I balk at that. "What, now you're a detective?"

"I spoke to a detective from the Chicago PD this morning."

"And he said they suspect her?"

Heaton's thin shoulders tense. "No. But she knows something, Daniel. She knows *everything*. She was the only one who saw the murderer. The police don't even have a description, which she could provide."

"Maybe she didn't see whomever it was. Maybe she's not ready."

Heaton shrinks back. "Not ready to identify her own sister's murderer?"

"I don't know. But I'm not rushing to judgment."

"Daniel, whoever came into Ava's apartment that night was *let* in. They were known to her and maybe to Allison, too. It wasn't a robbery gone bad, because Ava's autopsy report says she still had on her engagement ring when the autopsy was done. That ring was valued at more than fifty thousand dollars. Photos of it were published in online magazines. People knew about the value of the ring, but whoever came to her apartment that night had only one thing in mind—killing her. Whatever they said and did can help the police, but Allison won't cooperate."

"Dr. Heaton, let me remind you that your only obligation is to our patients. We aren't here to solve crimes or unnecessarily stress our patients for *any* reason."

"She's no more mentally ill than you or me, Daniel. I see complete realization and comprehension in her."

I scrub a hand over my face, my frustration mounting. "What the hell kind of psychiatrist are you? I specialized in emergency medicine, and even I know she could be suffering from a number of situational illnesses."

Heaton stands up. "I won't be treated this way. Lodge a formal complaint against me if you want to, but this conversation is over. I will treat Allison Cole, and all of my patients, as I see fit."

"You won't be seeing Allison anymore."

Her eyes are wide when she turns to me. "What? Why not?"

"She told me she doesn't want to do sessions with you anymore, and I agreed."

"She *told* you?" Heaton is aghast. "She *talks* to you, and you've never said anything about it?"

"She wrote me a message."

"That's still communication. You should have shared that with me."

"I just did."

"Well, she can write in our sessions if she prefers."

I shake my head. "There won't be any more sessions, Dr. Heaton. I'm honoring her request not to meet with you anymore."

"I've never . . ." Her voice shakes with anger, and she pauses before continuing. "The Hawthornes have given you too much power here. Patient care is supposed to be collaborative, but you're a dictator."

My laugh is humorless. "Well, that's a new one. Care is collaborative here, but one person has to be in charge. And I make calls with the patient's best interest in mind."

"What, and I don't?"

"You didn't today."

She narrows her eyes. "I *will* be taking this up with Joanne. We all have bosses, Daniel. Even you."

"Feel free to do that." I stand up and walk to the door, my hand on the knob when I turn to look at her over my shoulder. "I'll note the end of Allison's sessions with you on her chart."

I leave the room then, my shoulders tight with tension as I walk to my office. I'm so pissed at Heaton—way more so than I let on to her. Allison is being punished because Heaton crossed a line today. I can't do anything about that, but I can damn well make sure it never happens again.

When I get to my office, I close the door and sit down behind my desk, unable to find my focus. I know the doctor in me took up for Allison with Heaton. I'd do the same for any patient here. But this lingering sense of helplessness I feel isn't normal. I know that's not coming from the doctor in me, but from of the man who has feelings for Allison.

Though I haven't outwardly crossed a line with her, I have in my heart. And I feel like a fraud for coming down on Heaton over professional boundaries when they're looking pretty blurred to me right now, too. I have to keep my feelings for Allison in check, or they may start showing.

Chapter
NINE

I'VE BEEN BACK at Level Two for two weeks now, and it's hitting me harder than I thought it would. I hadn't realized how much I'd grown to love the wide-open Montana country and my hikes through the forest until they were taken away from me.

I've grown resentful, just sitting in the chair in my room all day and watching the others ride horses and walk through the clearing. I'm angry. Not at Dr. Heaton, as I probably ought to be, because I didn't expect anything more of her.

At first, my anger was directed at myself for not being able to withstand Dr. Heaton's antagonizing comments. She got to me, and she knows it. I hate that worse than I hate being a Level Two again.

In the past few days, though, I've started to get angry at Daniel. It's not a rational anger. He looks in on me most days, but it's just a casual stop in the doorway to ask if I'm good.

I want him to come into my room. I want him to look at me like he did that day when he helped me cross the creek. He hasn't returned *The Scarlet Letter* yet, and I want him to bring it in with a note tucked into the cover.

Mostly, I just want to know he hasn't forgotten me. I feel like we're back to a strict doctor-patient relationship, and I can't help wondering if my freak-out in Dr. Heaton's office isn't the reason.

"Hey, Allison." I turn to look at the doorway to my room, where Morgan is standing. "We're doing manicures downstairs, you should come."

I shake my head. She walks into the room and sits down on my bed.

"You can't just stay in here for a whole month. For one thing, it's not good for you, and for another, Tim keeps sitting next to me at dinner since you never come down for it. He cuts his food into equal-sized bites and then organizes it on his plate before he eats any of it. And he talks about math nonstop."

I don't even shake my head this time. Instead, I stare out the window, looking for a bird whose freedom I can daydream about. I'm not just physically trapped in this place; I'm also stuck inside my own head, where I have to fight against the memories that hurt my heart.

I'm completely alone in the world. Aunt Maggie hasn't visited me here or sent a letter. We were never close, and I'm sure she felt like she was doing me a solid just by bringing me here. I'm glad my mother didn't live to see what's become of her daughters— one murdered and the other a mute in a mental hospital. When she passed away three years ago from ovarian cancer, I thought I'd never feel another loss so profound. I was wrong. Foolishly, stupidly wrong.

And while Morgan is my friend, she's an eighteen-year-old whose world mostly revolves around herself.

"Okay, fine," she says, shrugging. "Come down if you change your mind, though. I like you better than Tim."

She gets up and leaves the room. I open the book I've been reading and return to it, hoping to lose myself in someone else's world for a while. My current mood has me reaching for darker reads, and I'm reading *1984* now.

The sky is just starting to shift toward sunset when I hear someone walking in the door with my dinner tray. It always arrives at 5:45 p.m.—fifteen minutes before dinner is served in the dining hall.

"Hey, I brought your dinner."

My stomach does a full flip as I turn to see Daniel standing in the doorway. Usually, a dining hall worker brings my tray. I close the book and set it down.

He sets the tray on the bed and walks back to the door. My heart sinks as I realize he's leaving. I want to call out and ask him to stay.

But when he puts his hand on the door, he closes it, staying in the room. He walks over and sits on the wide window ledge, just looking at me for a few seconds.

"I finished *The Scarlet Letter* a few days ago," he finally says. "Didn't bring it with me because . . ." He takes a deep breath. I've never seen him look anything but confident and in control until now. "I wasn't planning on coming here, but then . . . well, here I am."

He gestures at the tray of food on the bed. "If you want to eat while we talk . . . or while *I* talk, you know . . ."

I shake my head. I was mad at him when he walked into the room, but his nervousness is melting my anger. I hope he's not here to give me bad news, but I can't imagine why else he'd be nervous.

He looks at the cover of the book on my table, and the corners of his lips quirk up in a smile. "Well, shit. Things are worse than I thought."

I smile back, and his eyes lock on to mine for a long moment.

"If you're reading a book about remaining human in inhuman circumstances, I feel like I've failed you," he says. His dark eyes turn serious. "Will you tell me how you're feeling? On the board?"

I get up from the chair and pick up the dry-erase board and

marker from my nightstand. Then I sit down on the bed across from Daniel and write.

I miss being outside.

He nods. "Fifteen more days. I'm sorry you're stuck in here." I write another message.

It feels like you've been avoiding me.

He sighs softly and looks down at the ground. "I'm not gonna deny it. I have been. You have an effect on me, Allison. I'm not sure what to do with that."

I'm taken aback by his admission. I wipe the message off the board with a tissue, and we sit in silence for a minute.

When Daniel raises his head again, he says, "The next time you come to my office to return a book, go over to my bookcase and look at the picture in a frame on a stack of books. That's my son, Caleb. He's six."

Daniel has a son. I never imagined him with a family. And given that his son isn't here and his expression is pained, I know this is a tough subject for him. I try to reassure him with a look that whatever he's about to say, it's safe with me.

"I used to live in LA," he continues. "I worked at UCLA Medical Center. That's where I met my wife, Julie."

A wife. My heart constricts in my chest. He has a wife.

"She was a physical therapist there, and I was doing my residency. We dated for a while, then got married and had Caleb a year later. I was kind of a star on the rise in emergency medicine. I was getting good opportunities and advancing quickly. But the hours were intense. And to move up, I had to work even more. I wasn't home much."

Though his voice is distant, I can tell how hard it is for him to remember the things he's telling me. His expression is clouded with remorse.

"Julie and I weren't getting along. She wanted me to be a better husband and father, but I resented her for it. I felt like she disregarded all the work I'd put in to get where I was. She was right, of course . . . I should have tried harder. But I was too blinded by my own ambition. She left me, and I knew I'd failed my son, but it was too late. I started stopping at a bar near the hospital for a drink after work. Then it became four or five drinks."

He stands up, scrubbing a hand over his face. "Allison, I'm an alcoholic. It's been more than two years since my last drink, but I will always be an alcoholic. When I'm around alcohol, I can't control myself." He stares out the window, his expression forlorn. "When I was drinking, I did something I'm deeply ashamed of. It cost me my medical license for a year and finally made me realize I had to go to rehab. And once I got my license back, I came here. Hawthorne is in the middle of nowhere. Alcohol isn't allowed here. The nearest town is twenty miles away, and I don't have a car. That's deliberate. This is where I need to be to keep my demons at bay."

When he looks over at me, his dark eyes are swimming with emotion. "Do you understand what I'm saying?"

I nod, the pain in his eyes shattering my heart.

"I have to pour myself into this place," he says. "It keeps me sane. And I've never told anyone any of this, but I wanted you to know that there's always hope. There's always another path, even if it takes us someplace we never imagined being."

Forcing away the tears in my eyes, I write on the board.

Thank you for sharing that with me.

There's a hint of a smile on his lips. "You've already survived the worst, and you were fighting your way back up. I could see it. Don't let this thing with Heaton knock you back a single step.

Show her what you're made of."

I write another message below the first one.

I will.

He nods and looks at the dinner tray on the bed. "You want to eat that, or come down to the dining room with me?"

After wiping off the words on the board, I write on it.

I'll come down. Also, where is Caleb now?

Daniel's smile is sad. "Still in California. Julie got remarried a year ago. But Caleb came here to visit for a week last Christmas, and he's coming again next month. He's a great kid."

He nods toward the door. I lead the way, feeling his hand brush across my back right before we leave the room. It sends a warm shiver down my spine. That brief touch and Daniel's solid presence behind me provide all the reinforcement I need.

Chapter
TEN

MY MIND IS on Billy McGrath as I descend the main stairway and head across the great room for the elevator. The Level Three nurses called and told me he's been manic for almost twenty-four hours now, ranting in a language they don't understand and throwing himself against the walls of his room.

The poor kid's body has to be exhausted. I put in an order for some medicine to relax him, and I'm going up to check on him.

When I glance at a leather chair near the fireplace, I see Morgan brushing the long, shiny brown hair of someone sitting on the floor. My eyes immediately lock on to Allison, who gives me the slightest smile.

The light is back in her eyes now. She's been coming downstairs during the day and for dinner every night. Just this morning, I laughed when I read a note from her inside the cover of *Les Miserables*, the last book I gave her to read.

D,

I figured the title of this book was misspelled. Less Miserable sounded like a great choice for a mental patient. We can always use a pick-me-up, right? But it's not less miserable—it's depressing. Send me something happy next time.

A

PS—Caleb is a beautiful boy. He has your eyes.

I feel about ten feet tall for playing any part in bringing out that beautiful smile of hers. Telling her part of my past also shifted something inside me, and I feel a little less weighted down now. I'm seen as the leader here, the problem solver, the strong, level-headed doctor who usually has all the answers. But I'm just as fallible as anyone, and it felt good to admit my weaknesses to Allison and still see the shine of admiration for me in her eyes.

A wave of guilt sweeps through me for having these thoughts about a patient. And not just any patient, but one I'm treating at a mental hospital after she experienced severe trauma. No matter how I feel about her, Allison can never be anything more than a secret fantasy for me. I gave up self-indulgence a couple years ago when I checked in to rehab.

As I step on to the elevator, I try to shake it off. I have to be completely focused anytime I'm on Level Three. The Hawthorne staff still whispers about a doctor who was killed by a patient on Level Three in the 1960s. It was a brutal strangulation by a delusional man. At my size, I don't worry about being physically overwhelmed by a patient, but things can go wrong in other ways with the severity of the diagnoses up there.

When the elevator doors open on to Level Three, Sara is waiting for me, wearing the red scrubs of a Level Three nurse.

"I'm glad you're here," she says, laying a palm on my chest. "Billy's having some sort of break with reality. Dr. Tillman and Dr. Heaton are in with him now."

I ignore her touch and look down at Billy's chart on my tablet. "We don't know of anything specific triggering this, right?"

She shrugs helplessly. "With Billy, you never know."

I nod. "His episodes don't always have triggers."

It's times like this I wish I had a veteran mental health practitioner to rely on. When Joanne hired me, she said that between my experience and Heaton's, we could handle anything. But treating mental illness in an emergency room is much different than being a long-term caregiver, and I don't always agree with Heaton's approaches.

"He's locked down?" I ask Sara.

"Oh, yeah." Her eyes widen.

I turn to go into the room, and she calls out to me again. "Hey, are you going to the staff cookout this weekend?"

"If I'm around."

"Oh . . . well, I hope to see you."

"Yeah . . . maybe." I give her a tight smile.

I'm definitely not going. I wish I could get away for a long, solo hike this weekend, but if I did that, Tillman would have to miss the staff cookout. I'm planning to cover for him here so he can attend. I went to the cookout last year and regretted it. Sara got drunk and confessed her feelings for me. I'm not sure she even remembers, but it was uncomfortable for me.

Hell, it would be nice if I had any interest in hooking up with a nurse here to work out my sexual frustration. But I don't. The only woman I want is strictly off-limits.

I enter the code to get into Billy's room and see him curled up in a fetal position on the floor. Billy is one patient I wish I could do better by. Being a schizophrenic and an adolescent to boot has to be hard as hell.

Heaton is sitting in a chair, legs crossed. Tillman is sitting on the floor next to Billy, talking to him. He's using a soothing tone and a language I don't understand. Then he switches to English.

"We're at Hawthorne Hill, Billy. I'm Dr. Tillman. I gave you medicine to relax your body. You're safe. Take some deep breaths and let yourself sleep."

I'm momentarily stunned. Billy's eyes are locked on to Tillman, but they're starting to droop as he fades. Tillman is doing exactly what I'd be doing—maintaining enough distance to keep Billy from feeling threatened, but calming him.

Tillman speaks in the other language again, and this time, I recognize it as German. Billy reaches over and wraps his hand around Tillman's, and Tillman holds on to his hand until Billy drifts off to sleep.

"Help me move him into his bed?" Tillman says, turning to look at me.

"Sure."

Together, we lift Billy's limp body into the bed and cover him up. When I see the dark circles under his eyes, I wish I'd been called overnight to approve a medication order.

"He'll be out for a while," Tillman says in a low tone.

"Meet you in the hallway," I say, heading for the door.

"I need to update his chart, and then I'll be out."

Heaton leaves the room first, flashing me a dark look. She's still pissed I canceled her sessions with Allison. Why, I have no idea. Probably because she doesn't like not getting her way. But I'm not signing off on three hours a week of unproductive sessions that are stressful to a patient.

When Tillman walks out of the room, I give him a nod of acknowledgment.

"You handled that well," I say.

He doesn't look flattered by the compliment. "I'm thirty-nine years old. I've been practicing medicine longer than you have. And I'd appreciate you not being surprised that I'd handle a patient well."

I resist my urge to bite back. "You're right. But I'm thirty-five, not fresh out of med school. I can admit, though, that I didn't need to come up here."

The bitter expression fades from his face. "I get that you're in charge here, but I'm capable. I was taught that sedation can protect patients from themselves, and I'm working on being more progressive about that."

"So you need me to back off."

He nods. "I've been waiting for that since I came here, but it never happens. You're here seven days a week. When you go on those weekend camping trips with patients, you still round on Saturday morning and you come check up on me Sunday night. Weekends are supposed to be mine here."

I have to admit to myself that he's right. I do tend to want to know what's going on with the patients every day. And I also tend to believe no one knows them and their needs as well as me. I've probably been a little too hard on Tillman.

"Okay," I say, forcing the reluctance from my tone. "I get that. I'll start taking weekends off completely unless you need me."

"Thanks."

I sigh heavily. "And just so you know, it wasn't about you. This place is my way of keeping my mind off things sometimes, but I can see that I've been overstepping."

"You were also checking up on me."

His astute observation makes me smile. "Yeah, that too. But I can admit when I'm wrong."

"I think you need to have a talk with the Level Three nurses," he says. "Billy shouldn't have suffered through that manic episode for so long without medication. They should have paged one of us overnight."

"I agree. But why don't you handle it?"

"Okay."

"I had no idea you spoke German."

He shrugs. "Took it in college. I'm passable."

"I didn't know Billy spoke German, either."

Tillman's eyes widen. "He doesn't. Billy, that is. But which-ever personality that was apparently does. The human mind is fascinating."

"What was he saying?"

"Just now? He was asking me not to kill him when I first se-dated him, but once the meds kicked in, he asked me not to leave."

"I got another email from that doctor at a university in Cali-fornia asking if they can come do research on Billy. You think it's a good idea?"

Tillman shrugs. "I can see why they want to study him. We've documented eighteen distinct personalities. It would depend on their methods and his tolerance for them."

"Something to think about. We'd need to discuss it with his parents, too." I turn toward the elevator. "See you around."

When I get back down to the main level, I walk out a back door to see if Leonard's working on his garden. He's growing tomatoes because he thinks the government is collecting information on people's DNA through the ones we serve here.

There's no reason to lie to myself. I'll talk to Leonard for a few minutes if I see him, but I'm really taking a long route to my office to avoid seeing Allison. Every time my eyes meet hers, I have thoughts I feel guilty about soon after.

I've never struggled with feelings like this for a patient. When I worked in LA, I'd occasionally notice if a female patient was attractive, but I never would have acted on it, even when I was single. It's different with Allison. I'm drawn to her physically, but there's also something more.

That something more is what keeps me up at night thinking of her, and it's what's making me crave a shot of whiskey right now. I need a physical burn to overshadow the emotional one she makes me feel.

No matter how many days, months, and years I'm sober, I never forget the instant satisfaction my first drink of the day brought me. It was physical, mental . . . hell, sometimes it felt *spiritual*.

Yeah, if I had a bottle within reach, I'd be passed out drunk by nightfall.

The man everyone here thinks is strong definitely has his weaknesses.

Chapter
ELEVEN

FINALLY, MY THIRTY days back at Level Two are over. Morgan comes into my room the first morning and whoops with excitement when she sees me back in my regular clothes.

"You got paroled! Let's celebrate."

Her idea of a celebration starts with curling my hair. She carefully wraps it around her curling wand in pieces and then runs her fingers through it until it satisfies her. I don't look in the mirror to see how it turned out, because I never look in mirrors anymore. I've become adept at avoiding every mirror at Hawthorne Hill since every time I'd catch a glimpse of myself in one, I was reminded of my sister.

Morgan knows how much I missed horseback riding, so we go on a long ride, taking a wooded path that crosses the creek in a shallow spot and leads to a meadow of wild flowers.

I can't get enough of the sun and fresh air. It clears my mind of all the noise. Last night, I had the dream again, and it felt so real. The voice was more insistent than ever, urging me to come clean.

I've managed to move what happened from the front of my

mind, but it's always there in my subconscious. No matter where I go or how long I'm silent, I'll never outrun it. It's a crushing, overwhelming feeling.

"You excited about going camping with Dr. D this weekend?" Morgan asks me when we're almost back to the stable.

I nod and smile at her.

"I'm going too," she says, releasing her horse's reins to clap with excitement. "I traded weekends with Leonard so I could go with you. Dr. D only takes one or two people at a time."

She starts talking about Billy McGrath then, and I zone out. From what I've heard, Billy has lived at Hawthorne since he was a young child, and he'll probably live here his whole life. He's the son of a famous musician who put him here and never comes to visit.

I get sad when I think about that. Is Billy connected enough to reality to know his parents are apparently ashamed of him and don't care if they ever see him? Part of me hopes not.

My first night back at Level One, I'm everyone's favorite person because the head chef makes chocolate mousse for dessert. When I approach the table in the dining room where Morgan is sitting with Daniel and Leonard, I feel Daniel looking at me.

It's been a month since he's seen me out of the Level Two scrubs and in my own clothes, so maybe that's what has his attention. Or maybe it's my hair. I hope Morgan doesn't have me looking like a 1980s pop star.

The next day, I'm reading in the great room when I feel someone looking at me again, but the sensation isn't pleasant this time. Dr. Heaton is staring at me so hard it's unnerving. Much as I want to bury my face in my book again, I hold her gaze. I'm not scared of that bitch, and I want her to know it.

Though I'm sure I could be diagnosed with post-traumatic stress disorder, I'm not mentally ill in the way many patients at Hawthorne are. And the thought of Dr. Heaton pushing people in fragile mental states the way she pushed me that day . . . well, it enrages me. She's on a power trip of some sort.

As soon as she's out of sight, I go to my room and write a note to Daniel, folding it in half and taking it to his office immediately.

I expected him to be rounding on patients, but he's in the chair behind his desk when I walk into the office, wearing his reading glasses and typing on a laptop.

"Allison . . . hey," he says, closing the screen. "Come on in. Have a seat."

I wonder if Daniel knows how much it means to me that he treats me like a normal person. He doesn't make my silence into an awkward issue or make it his mission to solve it. This is how doctors should make patients feel.

I pass him the note and then sit down in a chair in front of his desk. There's a mischievous gleam in his eyes as he looks at the folded paper and then up at me, but he quickly clears his throat and schools his expression into a more serious one.

As he opens the note and reads it, I read it back to myself in my head.

I'm ready to go back to my sessions with Dr. Heaton now. Thanks for letting me take a break.

He pinches his brows together and looks at me. "You don't have to do that. If those sessions aren't working for you, you never have to go back."

I point at the note, resolved. Daniel nods, folds it in half again, and sets it aside. "Okay. I'll arrange it."

I stand up and turn to leave the office.

"Hey, is there anything else you want to talk about?"

That makes me smile. He laughs and runs a hand down his five o'clock shadow.

"I mean . . . as *we* talk, you know? You can write, or pantomime if you want. Interpretive dance, maybe?"

My smile widens. He's a giant of a man—his shoulders have to be twice as wide as mine, and he's around six and a half feet tall—and that makes his soft side dangerously cute.

I shake my head and he leans back in his chair, looking relaxed. "So, for our camping trip tomorrow night . . . pack light. Our campsite's a five-mile hike. I'll have all the essentials in my pack."

Just the thought of a night in the woods makes me smile. It'll be a first for me, but then, everything else at Hawthorne has been a first for me, too. I don't think I could keep breathing if my new life wasn't different in every way from my old one. The memories cut deep even when they're just buried in my heart. Other reminders would ruin me.

"Guess I'll see you in the morning," Daniel says. "I won't make it to dinner in the dining room tonight because I have reports to finish."

Our eyes lock and I lick my lips, my mouth suddenly feeling dry all over. We don't always share a table in the dining room, but there's something about him telling me he won't be there tonight that I like. But not as much as I like the idea of spending two days in the woods with him. And of course, Morgan. For a second there, I completely forgot about her.

"HE SAYS I can't go on the camping trip."

Morgan is near tears when I walk down the main staircase the next morning. She's sitting on a couch in the great room with one foot on the coffee table.

Daniel is standing next to the coffee table, his arms crossed. His expression is a mix of concern and amusement.

"I really think I'll be fine," Morgan says, putting on a confident smile. "It feels much better now."

"That's because your weight's not on it anymore. It's definitely sprained, Morgan. You can't even walk across this room right now, much less five miles into the woods."

"But I want to go. I traded with Leonard so Allison and I could go camping together."

"There'll be other times," Daniel tells her.

She sits back against the leather couch and huffs out a sigh. "This sucks."

"It does," Daniel says. "But considering that you fell down the entire staircase, I'm just glad you didn't hurt yourself any worse."

He looks over at me as I join them. "She was carrying her backpack downstairs, and she missed the top step. Scared the sh . . . uh, crap out of me."

"You can say shit, Dr. D," Morgan says in a sulky tone. "This is definitely an occasion for the word shit." She looks up at me from the couch. "You should still go. Don't stay here just because of me."

I sit down next to her and wrap my arm around her shoulders. She leans her head on me and sighs heavily.

"I know it's disappointing, Morgan," Daniel says. "How about if we hike all the way to that waterfall you like when you're able to camp again?"

She lifts her head. "Yeah? Okay. When will that be?"

Daniel looks down at her ankle, which is swollen to twice its usual size. "Well, let's see how it goes. Dr. Tillman will come take a look when he finishes rounding."

Sara, the nurse who has the hots for Daniel, comes out of the kitchen with an ice pack and hands it to Daniel, deliberately brushing her hand across his.

"Anything else I can do to help?" she asks sweetly.

Daniel bends down to put the ice on Morgan's swollen ankle. "Yeah, will you find Leonard and ask him if he still wants to go camping? Tell him we're moving out in ten minutes."

"Sure, no problem."

Ugh. She's so bubbly and compliant. I immediately dislike her. I guess it might have something to do with her obvious feelings for Daniel.

What if he's seeing her? The thought makes my stomach roll. But he lives in the middle of nowhere at a mental hospital, so his options are very limited.

I'm still stewing when Sara returns a couple minutes later.

"Leonard says he can't go because he's helping at the stables this afternoon."

"Oh." There's a note of disappointment in Daniel's voice. "Okay, thanks."

"Anything else you need?" Sara asks him, putting her hand on his back. "Anything at all?"

I roll my eyes at her overenthusiasm. Daniel shakes his head, not looking at her from his seat on the coffee table.

"Morgan, do you want to stay here or go back to your room?" he asks. "I can carry you to your room if you want me to."

Morgan shrugs. "Might as well stay here."

"Can you have someone bring her breakfast out here?" Daniel asks Sara, standing up.

"I sure will. What about you? Did you have breakfast? Can I get you something?"

"Nah, we're good." Daniel looks over at me. "You ready?"

I nod and give Morgan a quick hug.

"Guess I don't have to worry about you making me jealous with stories about how great it was," she says with a weak smile.

"Bye, guys," Daniel says, picking up a giant backpack and swinging it over one shoulder.

He's wearing a T-shirt and dark cargo pants, and the muscles on his arms ripple as he settles the second shoulder strap of the pack. Sara is practically drooling, and I can't say I blame her.

With his inked arms and hiking boots, Daniel doesn't look

like a doctor today. He looks more like a hot lumberjack I'd like to get lost in the woods with.

The chances are slim, though. He knows these woods like the back of his hand. As he leads me deeper into the forest and Hawthorne Hill disappears from view, I feel a rush of excitement over being alone with him here, in the place he loves most. He doesn't even have to say it; I can tell he's most comfortable in the outdoors. He moves differently here. His expression is open, the weight of responsibility gone.

We hike the first couple miles in silence. We're taking a different path than the one I've been on for hikes, and this one has lots of incline around the third mile.

"Doing okay?" Daniel asks at the top of a steep climb, passing me a bottle of water.

I nod and take several sips.

"We've got some light climbing ahead, but I'll help you if you need it." He grins. "I can't usually come to this campsite unless I'm alone, because most patients aren't fit enough to hike to it."

All those spin classes I did back home were worth it. I'm not in the same shape I was when I got here, but I know I can handle this hike. Will I be sore tomorrow? Hell yes, but it'll be worth it. I like knowing we're going somewhere he usually only goes alone.

Daniel finishes his water, crushes the bottle in his hand, and then packs his bottle and mine into his pack, and we start walking again.

He wasn't kidding about the climbing. We have to scale a small stretch of rock, and it's all I can do to hold on. Daniel climbs up right behind me, somehow managing to stay on the rock even when I slip and he has to hold my weight, too.

"Almost there," he says, his breath hot against my neck. "There's a tree trunk at the top, and once you get a good hold on it, I'll boost you up over the edge."

I'm struggling for breath as I grab the trunk and try to haul myself up. I only make it a few inches and then I feel Daniel's hand on my ass, pushing me up far enough that I can climb the rest of the way over.

He pulls himself over next, and he's grinning sheepishly as he takes in several deep breaths at the top.

"Sorry," he says. "I didn't mean to . . . there was no other way I could get you over with this pack on my back."

I smile back and arch my brows, hoping he can tell that I didn't mind his hand on my ass at all.

He slides his pack off and sits down, patting the ground beside him. I sit down, and he gets out water and trail mix.

"So I've got a question for you," he says. "You don't have to answer it unless you want to."

I nod, take off my baseball cap, and comb my hands through my hair, refastening it into a ponytail and putting the hat back on.

"Are you physically able to talk?"

Our eyes meet, and I see such genuine curiosity in his that I can't not answer him. When I nod, he nods back.

"That's good. I figured as much, but I didn't want to assume. Your vocal cords could have been damaged by . . ." He clears his throat and looks around. "It's pretty up here, don't you think? This is one of my favorite spots."

I look up at the branches of the tall trees creating a full canopy from the sun. It *is* beautiful. I feel like Daniel and I are the only two people in the world right now.

"Alone with you for a night," he says softly, then laughs. "I thought we'd have Morgan chattering in between us all night long in the tent."

The nervousness in his tone touches and excites me at the same time. He *does* feel something. Before I can overthink it, I reach for his hand and entwine our fingers. For an instant, he stiffens, but then his hand closes around mine and he brings my hand up to his lips. He brushes his lips over the back of my hand, the gentle scrape of his stubble making me tingle.

"I wish we'd met at a different time and place," he murmurs, closing his eyes.

I wish I could tell him that we were meant to meet at this time. In this place. I needed Daniel when I got here, as much as I've ever needed anyone. He's helped me more than I'll ever be able to tell him.

"We should get back to it," he says, releasing my hand. "Before I do something really stupid."

He gets up and then offers me a hand. And when he helps me up, he pulls me closer to him. I like feeling the warmth of his body and seeing desire in his eyes when I look up at him. Desire for *me*.

When he releases my hand and starts walking again, I know for sure he's not seeing Sara or anyone else. There was such hunger in his expression that I can tell he hasn't been with a woman in a long time. And God, how I'd love to end his dry spell.

Chapter
TWELVE

THE CAMPFIRE CRACKLES with satisfaction as I toss another log and some dried grass onto it. I sit down on a stump and hunch forward, elbows on my knees.

I'm fucking exhausted. I haven't stopped moving all day because being around Allison makes me feel like a stick of dynamite on the edge of exploding. After the hike to the campsite, I pitched the tent, made spears from sticks, went fishing, and chopped firewood.

There's a small shed nearby that's full of fishing supplies. Rods and reels would have been a hell of a lot easier than whittling spears and using them was. So why did I do it?

I want Allison. I want to take her into the tent, peel off her clothes, and fuck her slow and hard. I want the first sound I hear from her to be a moan of satisfaction she can't hold back as I make her come. It's one thing to want it inside the privacy of my own head, but it's getting harder to hide it from her.

All she did on the way to the campsite was reach for my hand, but that small gesture has me worked up for her. Does she want my comfort—or something more? I'd find it difficult to deny her anything she wanted from me.

It was stupid of me to bring her out here by herself. I might as well have brought a bottle of Jack and told myself I wouldn't open it.

So I fished and chopped and wore my body down to a point of relaxation. And as soon as Allison walks out of the tent and smiles at me, my dick twitches in response. Damn. That part of me is definitely not exhausted.

She picks up one of the spears I left leaning against a tree, running her fingertips over the smooth, pointed end. Watching her gives me a full-on erection.

I look at the fire so I can get rid of my hard-on before I stand up to cook dinner. The woods are dimming as the sun sets, and it'll be dark by the time the food is ready.

Allison walks over just as I get up. She looks at ease out here, like she's spent lots of time in the woods. I wish I could talk to her about that . . . and so many other things. It's crazy that I feel so close to a woman who's never said a single word to me.

"You want to help with dinner?" I ask her.

She nods and I unpack cooking supplies and food from my pack. Soon she's peeling potatoes and I'm cleaning fish. The humming and singing of the forest make for tranquil background noise as we work.

When it's time to cook, she watches me, and I get the sense she hasn't done much cooking before. I add oil to the skillet I brought and season the fish and potatoes before putting in the first batch.

"There's a cabin a few miles deeper into the woods," I tell her. "Henry Hawthorne had it built so he'd have a place to stay when he went hunting. I found some journals and photos in a file cabinet at Hawthorne once about what an undertaking it was for the workers. Henry wouldn't allow any clearing of the forest for it, so they had to carry everything ten miles into the woods."

There's a sparkle of interest in her brown eyes when they meet mine.

"Maybe we can camp there next time," I say.

She smiles, and it hits me just how much I like being the one to make her smile. I like it way more than I should, but too much to be sorry about.

When the food is done cooking, I give her a sheepish smile. "I'm so used to camping by myself that I didn't bring plates. I just eat out of the pan." I hand her the fork I brought, and I use my big cooking spoon.

We eat, and she nods enthusiastically when I ask if she likes it. By her expression, I think she really does. Whether it's from the hunger of only eating trail mix and fruit until now, I don't even care. I made her dinner and she likes it. It's as close to a date as we'll ever get.

I cooked a shitload of food, and we finish almost all of it. Allison gets out her dry-erase board and writes out a message offering to go wash the dishes, but I tell her I'll do it. I grab a bar of soap and wash myself off at the stream I rinse the dishes in, conscious of smelling like sweat. I change into a clean shirt and head back to our campground, where Allison is sitting by the fire with a blanket around her shoulders.

There's a chill in the air tonight. I can think of a few great ways to stay warm. More than warm, actually. We'd both be hot and sweaty in no time.

Allison looks up at me when I approach, and I wonder if my dirty thoughts about her are written on my face. She lifts an arm, opening the blanket to me.

"You cold?" I ask her.

She nods, and I forget my warring thoughts about what I should and shouldn't do. I want to be close to her, and she wants it, too. Just this once, I want to give in to what feels good.

I sit down next to her and take the blanket, wrapping it around both of us and pulling her against me with an arm around her shoulders. She snuggles into me and sighs softly.

"You took off the hat," I say, brushing my lips over the top of her head.

Her hair is soft and it has a light, sweet scent. I'm breathing her in when she wraps her arms around my waist and holds on to me tightly.

"You make it so easy to forget," I murmur.

She lifts her head from my chest and looks up at me, and I can read enough of her expression in the light of the fire to know she feels the same. I run a hand over her hair, then cup her cheek, which is tiny in my massive hand.

"I forget what's right." I brush my thumb across her cheekbone. "I forget why I'm here." I tighten the hold of my other arm around her. "I forget how I've failed in the past." I close my eyes and sigh, resting my forehead against hers. "I forget that you're fragile."

She moves then, and I open my eyes. Allison is climbing into my lap, straddling my waist. We're chest to chest, her knees on either side of my thighs. I wrap my arms around her back, her soft body molding against mine. When she brushes a hand over my cheek and then around to the back of my neck, her eyes tell me she's anything but fragile in this moment.

I brush my mouth over hers in a gentle kiss, and she parts her lips, silently seeking more. Holding her close, I give it to her, kissing her deeper and harder. She shifts her hips just enough to make me groan from the friction of her rubbing against my erection.

When I pull back, she rests her forehead against mine, her breath warm on my lips as she pants slightly.

"It's like getting drunk," I murmur. "You give me the same fuzzy high I got from booze. I've never . . . *fuck*."

Desire swirls hot and thick between us, the cold night air

forgotten. Allison has woken something inside of me that's been asleep for a long time, and I don't know if I have enough willpower to resist the pull I feel.

A deep howling sound close by makes Allison turn, her body stiffening with worry.

"It's okay," I say. "Nothing's gonna bother us here."

She's still staring into the dark woods, so I ease her off my lap and ask, "You want to go in the tent?"

She turns her head quickly, meeting my gaze and nodding. The warm hope swirling in her brown eyes makes me groan again.

"I can't . . . I mean, *we* can't . . ." I shake my head. "You're my patient, Allison. I have to respect that boundary, no matter how much I want you."

She walks a few feet to get her dry-erase board, writing out a message and turning the board to face me.

I'm not crazy.

Her earnest expression tugs at me.

"I know. I've never thought you were crazy. I think you're experiencing post-traumatic stress disorder, which is completely understandable. Even if I weren't your doctor, I just . . ." I sigh heavily. "But I am."

She nods and I see both understanding and disappointment in her eyes. When she turns and walks to the tent, I follow. She crawls inside, and I stick my head through the tent flaps.

"Hey, it's good to change clothes before bed. Clothes retain moisture even if you don't feel it, and you'll be warmer in dry clothes. You can change in there, and I'll change out here."

As soon as I stand and walk over to my pack, I smile to myself as I realize I already changed when I was down by the stream. Allison has quite an effect on me.

I give her more than enough time to change, because I've only got so much self-control, and seeing her partially undressed would unravel me. After a few minutes, I take two bottles of water, my shotgun, and some shells from my pack and climb into the tent.

She's lying on top of her sleeping bag, wearing black cotton pants and a long-sleeve gray T-shirt, her hair in a loose bun on top of her head.

I pass her a bottle of water and unzip both sleeping bags.

"We could, uh . . . both lie on one of these and cover up with the other one," I suggest, saying the words before I have time to talk myself out of it. "If you want."

Her lips curve up in a smile, and she moves off her sleeping bag to help me rearrange them. A couple minutes later, we're side by side in the darkness. It feels nice, just having her this close.

Allison slides her head beneath my arm and snuggles against me. I wrap my arm around her back, trying to ignore how much I want more than this.

"We're fully clothed. There's nothing wrong with this," I say. "Leonard and I sleep like this when we camp, actually."

She laughs. It's just a slight sound I'm sure she meant to hold back but couldn't. Even though she didn't talk, I got something. I can tell her voice is sweet and sexy just from that taste.

"We spoon, actually," I say. "Leonard in back, of course."

This time, she laughs against my shirt, the sound muffled. I smile in the darkness, still loving it.

"Hey, if you need anything during the night, wake me up," I say, brushing my lips across her forehead. "Don't leave the tent without me for any reason. I've got my shotgun in here just in case, but I don't think we'll have any issues with animals."

She nods against me, running her palm over my chest through my T-shirt. I close my eyes, savoring the way this feels. We may never get another night like this—just the two of us, alone and away from Hawthorne. Tonight I broke the trust the Hawthorne administration puts in me by letting me take patients camping. My integrity has never been in question with them. But I can't quite bring myself to be sorry right now.

I'd stay awake all night if I could, but as soon as Allison's breathing evens out, I pull the top sleeping bag around us and start drifting off myself.

In another life, we could have more than this. We'd *be* so much more than this. I'd let myself free-fall for the dark-haired woman who mesmerizes me without saying a single word. I'd be her comfort, and she'd be my salvation.

But this life is reality. I'm her doctor, and I suspect she won't be at Hawthorne forever. Once she learns to cope with what happened to her sister, she'll be able to start a new life somewhere else. Eventually, with *someone* else, I'm sure. She's too incredible to be overlooked.

This is the only time I've ever wished one of my patients wouldn't make a full recovery as soon as they possibly could.

Chapter
THIRTEEN

THE SOUND OF movement next to me jolts me awake.

"It's okay," Daniel says softly. "It's just me."

I look around the tent, remember we're camping, and let my head fall back to my sleeping bag. When I give him an apologetic look, Daniel looks sheepish.

"It's my fault for waking you up," he says. "I was trying to sneak out so I could have breakfast ready when you woke up."

He's leaning up on one elbow, and I pat his sleeping bag, encouraging him to stay in the tent a bit longer. He does one better, pulling me closer and wrapping his arms around me.

I close my eyes, pressing my cheek to his chest. I was having a dream when I woke up, and it wasn't the usual one with the strange man prodding me to tell him the details of that terrible night.

This dream was about two dark-haired little girls playing beneath a tent they'd made from a bedsheet in their playroom. The smiles and laughter had felt so real—probably because they *were* real, many years ago. We'd been inseparable until I made a bad decision that drove a wedge between us. But even then, I'd never even imagined a world without my beautiful, vibrant twin in it.

"You okay?" Daniel asks, his stubble tickling my temple as his lips brush across it.

I nod against his chest, pushing the dream from my mind. The singing and croaking sounds from the woods are a beautiful wake-up call. I soak in my surroundings for a few seconds before sitting up.

"I can't remember the last time I slept so well," Daniel says with a sleepy smile. "Did you sleep okay?"

I nod, feeling wistful as I look at him. His dark hair is rumpled, and his expression has lazy Sunday morning written all over it. In another time and place, we'd spend the next few hours in bed. Or maybe the entire day, only leaving for the essentials.

In a way, he's all mine right now. But in the only way that truly matters, he never can be.

"You're beautiful," he says, reaching for my hand. I smile as he entwines our fingers.

"What do you want to do today? Just nod when I get to something that sounds good. We can go fly fishing, hiking, climbing, canoeing—"

I nod and he gives me a sexy grin.

"Canoeing, huh? Are you a strong swimmer?"

I nod again.

"You'll have to wear a life jacket anyway. I've got some in the supply shed."

We leave the tent then, going to the very primitive outhouse not far from camp. It's pretty much a deep hole in the ground with two walls, but it's better than nothing.

Daniel fixes more potatoes, this time, mixing in mushrooms and peppers he brought. It's like an omelet without eggs, and it's not bad. We roll up our sleeping bags and pack up the tent, and I realize we probably won't get to come out here alone again. I wish we could, but I'm grateful we at least had one night alone. Now I know Daniel has feelings for me, even if he can't act on them. He doesn't see me as a crazy person. Even if everyone else at Hawthorne thinks I'm unbalanced, the one person who matters sees the real me.

It takes about an hour to hike to the lake we're canoeing at. There's a small shed on one bank, and the canoe is sitting next to it, looking like it hasn't seen water in a while.

We empty out the leaves, and Daniel opens the woodshed to get out some supplies. He puts a life jacket on me, a smile playing on his lips as he fastens the straps.

"I may accidentally touch you while I'm doing this," he says, his fingers brushing down the side of one of my breasts in a very *non-accidental* way.

I don't know if it's his touch making me break out in goose bumps, or the desire flaring in his eyes. There's a realization deep inside me, and it's bittersweet. Daniel doesn't just find me attractive. I'm not "fuckable," as some of my male college friends sometimes described women.

There's something much more than that between us. This yearning doesn't come so much from my body as from my soul. No man has ever looked at me this way—with such deep longing to have me just as I am. Even when I had a lot more going for me, I never felt as *worthy* as I do with Daniel.

He takes my hand as I step into the canoe and sit down, then steps in himself, pushes the canoe away from the shore, and sits down.

The water ripples as the boat cuts through it, and I like its smooth, swirling sound. Daniel puts the oars into the water, the lines of his arm muscles standing out beneath his gray T-shirt as he rows.

"I'd recite poetry for you if I knew any," he says with a grin.

"I only know the ones I learned in the army, and they're not fit for a lady's ears."

I arch my brows with amusement and motion toward myself with one hand, telling him to spill his so-called poem. He laughs as he pushes the oars through the lake's water, the canoe moving at a nice clip thanks to the biceps I'm still admiring.

"You asked for it," he says, then clears his throat. "There once was a girl named Sapphire, who gave in to her lover's desire. She said, 'It's a sin, but now that it's in, could you shove it a few inches higher?'"

I throw my head back, silently laughing.

"We had too much time on our hands sometimes," he says. "Dirty jokes and card games kept us busy. And then when we were in the field, there was never enough time. Funny how that is, isn't it?"

I sigh softly, thinking about how little I find funny anymore. I still feel like I'm surviving more than actually living. It's only been a few months since I laughed so hard my stomach hurt, but it seems like a lifetime ago.

When I reach for the oars, meeting Daniel's gaze in an offer to help with the rowing, a corner of his mouth lifts in a grin.

"I've got it."

I put my hands back on the narrow wooden seat, watching him row. His physical presence, which felt overwhelming the first time I saw him, is the source of my fantasies and my comfort now that I know him. The muscles he hones climbing in these woods are sexy, but I wonder if he's always had this body. Did Caleb's mother rest her head on his chest the way I did last night, falling asleep with his hard arms wrapped around her?

She probably did, many times. How many women has Daniel been with? As careful and considerate as he's been with me, I sense a restless soul in him. Someone who went looking for life's answers in all the wrong places when he was younger, and that probably included lots of sex.

"What's on your mind?" He arches his brows in question. "Wishing Morgan were here?"

By his smile, I know he already knows the answer, but I shake my head anyway. Then I turn my face up to the clear blue sky, closing my eyes to enjoy the feel of the warm sun on my skin. I missed it during my thirty days at Level Two.

Daniel rows in silence until we reach a small island. He hops out of the canoe, his boots splashing in the water, and pulls it all the way ashore before helping me out.

I sit on the grassy bank and look out over the water. The mountain range in the distance draws my attention, because seeing mountains still feels unreal. The majesty of this place reminds me there's a big, beautiful world around me. People experience grief and joy and everything in between every hour of every day. There's something very comforting about that.

Daniel gathers a small pile of smooth, flat rocks. He flicks his wrist as he tosses one over the surface of the lake, and we both watch as it skips in and out of the water several times before sinking.

When he does it again, I can't deny I'm a little impressed. He offers me a rock, and I stand up and take it.

Even after watching him skip several more stones, I can't make mine do anything but sink straight to the bottom of the lake. My frustration is minimal, though. I think it's because of the way Daniel is looking at me, his brown eyes warm and full of affection.

We explore the wooded island a bit more before returning to the canoe. Daniel tells me more about his time in the army and how it shaped him. He talks a bit about his parents, who live in Spain. The one subject he avoids is his ex-wife and son. I know it's painful for him, and I also know all about avoiding things that hurt so deeply that you aren't ready to confront them.

Early in the afternoon, we start the hike back to Hawthorne

Hill. We walk mostly in silence, taking our time. The physical exertion is soothing. I can see why Daniel likes it out here so much.

When we get to the tree line and can see the main Hawthorne building, Daniel stops and tugs lightly on my ponytail.

"I had a really good time," he says. "I hope you did, too."

I nod, the look in his eyes making me warm all over. I want him to kiss me, but he doesn't. We're too close to Hawthorne—too close to reality.

When we walk through the tall double doors of the main lodge, Daniel shrugs off his heavy pack and sets it on the floor, helping me get my much smaller one off, too.

"I'll make us something to eat," he says, turning toward the kitchen.

He doesn't make it far before Leonard comes flying into the room, clearly upset. There's a nurse behind him, and from her expression, I can tell something's going on.

"You think I did it, don't you?" Leonard's accusing tone is directed at Daniel.

"Hey, Leonard," Daniel says. "How's it going?"

Leonard's brow is furrowed angrily. "You think I did it. You're no better than the rest of them."

"What do you mean? Think you did what?"

Leonard scoffs and shakes his head. "Don't play dumb with me. You know what I'm talkin' about. She thinks the same damn thing." He gestures toward me.

Daniel says, "I don't, actually. Can you tell me?"

Narrowing his eyes, Leonard says, "JFK. You think I planned the whole thing."

"I don't think that," Daniel says in a level tone. "Neither does Allison."

Leonard turns back to me. "That true?"

I nod, but he just shakes his head.

"This is a bunch of bullshit right here," he says, agitated. "You think I'm gonna go to sleep so you can tie me up and haul me off to prison and no one will ever know. I won't, though."

"Leonard, can we sit down and talk?" Daniel asks.

Leonard gives him a wary look. I slip away so Daniel can talk to him in private. I feel bad for Leonard, because I could tell he truly believed what he was saying. It has to be scary to genuinely believe something like that.

The more I see what Daniel does here, the more my admiration for him grows. He's off today. He could have let Dr. Tillman or that nurse handle Leonard, but he wanted to do it himself. His compassion is one of the reasons I feel myself falling for him.

There's no hope for a real relationship between us, but that doesn't change the way I feel.

I take a long, hot shower, and while it feels good to get clean, I also feel a twinge of regret. I'm washing away the feel of Daniel's hands on me. It will only exist in my dreams now. And even then, that's only if I can manage to dream about something pleasant for once.

Chapter FOURTEEN

I TAKE LEONARD into my office, turning the two chairs in front of my desk so they're facing each other.

"Am I under arrest?" Leonard asks bitterly. "Is that what this is?"

"No. I just want to talk to you. It's okay, go ahead and sit down."

He gives me a wary look but finally sits. I sit across from him.

"Leonard, you're at Hawthorne Hill. It's a hospital."

"I know that," he shoots off. "It's all part of the plan to frame me."

"No. You're here because sometimes your mind makes you believe things that aren't real. I'm Dr. Delgado, and I'm treating you. I've got you on an antipsychotic medication, but sometimes, the thoughts come back anyway."

He just stares at me in silence.

"And when that happens, we talk about it. Can you remember having this kind of conversation with me before?"

"I don't know . . . maybe." He looks toward the window.

"These thoughts you have, they're not your fault. They seem

real. And I know that makes you feel scared."

"I ain't scared of shit."

I force myself not to smile. "Do you know that I'm Dr. Daniel Delgado and we're at Hawthorne Hill?"

"Yeah, I know that."

"Good. Sometimes when you're struggling with these thoughts, horseback riding helps. Do you want to go riding?"

He crosses his arms and sighs heavily. "Stable's closed on weekends."

"We can make an exception for you."

Though he doesn't respond, I see the wheels turning in his mind. He knows I'm telling him the truth, which means he knows he's paranoid. When I have this conversation with him, there's never relief on his part. He's a proud man, and it crushes him to realize he's creating delusions.

"You okay now?" I ask him.

He nods.

"Mind if I come for a ride with you?"

"'Course not, Doc."

"Meet me out in the great room. I'm gonna grab a sandwich to eat on the way."

Leonard leaves and I text Tillman, who tells me he's on Level Two. Five minutes later, he walks into my office.

"Hey," he says, dropping into a chair.

"Hey. Just wanted to let you know I'm taking Leonard out riding. He's having some paranoia again."

Tillman sighs heavily. "Yeah, Eric paged me last night because Leonard was pretty upset. He was threatening to jump out a window."

"Eric?"

"The night shift CNA on Level One. You know, the big guy."

"Oh, right. He knows the windows here are too thick to be

broken, doesn't he?"

"Yeah, but he couldn't calm Leonard down."

"Did you sedate him?"

Tillman cocks a brow at me. "No. I've been waiting to see if the mania subsides on its own. But Level Three has been keeping me busy today, so I've got a nurse keeping an eye on him."

He's got dark circles under his eyes. I feel like an asshole for going horseback riding when Tillman's overwhelmed.

"How long have you been working?" I ask him.

He shrugs. "I got the page at two in the morning."

I look at the clock on my wall. It's almost 4:00 p.m. "You want me to take over so you can get some sleep?"

"No, I'm fine. I've worked long shifts before. Coffee keeps me going."

"Okay."

He gets up to leave, and I remember something. "Hey, can you cover me for the last week of July?"

"Sure. You finally taking a vacation?"

"Kind of. My son's coming for a visit."

"Take him somewhere if you want. Go to Disneyworld or something."

I smile. "Caleb likes it here. He loves horseback riding and camping."

Tillman shrugs. "Well, consider yourself off that week. Though I'm sure you'll check up on me daily."

I don't respond to his jab. "Thanks, man."

He leaves my office, and I go into the kitchen to make a sandwich. When I go into the great room to meet Leonard, I can't help scanning it for Allison.

Ten minutes apart and I'm already missing her. Kissing her last night shifted things from attraction to something more. Not that I can act on it.

"You ready, Doc?" Leonard asks me.

"Yeah, let's go."

We head for the side entrance that leads to the trail to the stable. I sneak one last glance at the stairs to see if Allison's coming down.

I can't believe I've got such strong feelings for a patient. I am well and truly fucked.

Chapter
FIFTEEN

THE NEXT COUPLE weeks pass slowly. Things at Hawthorne are as good as they can be—there's a new twenty-year-old male patient, Milo, that Morgan has a crush on, and I manage to pass my weekly sessions with Heaton without so much as a cringe. The more incendiary her comments are, the more impassive I act.

Outwardly, anyway. Inside, I'd like to punch her in the throat. She's the least therapeutic therapist ever. But at least now I know she's going to try to push my buttons in every session.

Time crawls by because of Daniel. I've had no reason to be alone with him since our camping trip. We've exchanged a few books and he's left notes inside them that made me smile, and I've felt him looking at me on more than one occasion. The intensity in his expression is enough to make my pulse pound, even when he's across the room.

It's agonizing being so close to him, but not getting a moment alone. At an impromptu staff and patient cookout, I had to watch that nurse Sara touch his bicep every time he said something that made her laugh, which was roughly every thirty seconds. I ended up dumping my plate in the garbage and going up to my room to read.

Pretending to be indifferent toward him gets even harder when I see him with Caleb. Daniel's son has his dark hair and caramel-colored eyes. He's a happy boy who obviously adores his father. When I watch them horseback riding and heading off to the woods on fishing trips, I feel a powerful pull toward Daniel.

He brings Caleb to the Hawthorne dining hall for dinner every night, and everyone loves having a child around. Everyone wants to sit by them, and I guess it's for the best that I end up at another table with Morgan every night. Getting attached to Caleb won't end any better for me than getting attached to Daniel will.

I'm already grouchy over missing Daniel when I go into Dr. Heaton's office for my appointment. She's wearing gray pants, a white blouse, and dark heels, her hair pulled back in its usual knot.

"Hello, Allison," she says from her desk. "Come on in and sit down."

I take a seat on her couch, looking out the window for birds I can focus on when her interrogation starts. She's writing something at her desk, and I've spotted eight birds by the time she gets up and comes over.

"Anything special you want to talk about this week?" she asks, looking at me as she sits down across from me.

I hold her gaze for a few seconds, until she speaks again. "So your aunt Margaret called yesterday to check up on you. She'd really love for you to get better and come to Manhattan for a visit."

My aunt Maggie only called to ease her conscience, I'm sure. Since my mom died, she's tried to check in regularly with phone calls, but she's busy with her own life. We've never been close.

"You come from a family with money," Dr. Heaton says, her brow furrowed. "Don't you want to get your life back? You can travel. Live anywhere you want. Surely you don't want to be cooped up in a mental hospital."

I turn toward the window and spot a gray bird with its wings spread wide. That's where I want to be right now—outside. Not necessarily free of Hawthorne Hill, but free of this office. Free of the trickling fountain and ticking wall clock.

"Come on, Allison." Now she's turned on her friendly tone. "We both know you don't belong here. You're no more mentally ill than I am."

She has an arsenal of tactics that seems endless. When one doesn't work, she pulls out another. I stare at the bird, determined to sit here for an hour without showing any reaction. That's how I get to her, which I enjoy immensely.

"You don't want to help the police find Ava's murderer. You don't want your own freedom. But there has to be *something* you want. So what is it? Say it, write it down . . . have it skywritten if you'd like. Just give me something to work with."

I sigh softly and sit back on the couch, fluffing the cushion on the end. She really hates it when I act like she's not even here.

Dr. Heaton leans forward in her chair. "Why don't we start with this, then? Where's the book, Allison?"

A chill travels down my spine as I meet her eyes. What the hell did she just say?

The corners of her lips curl into a slight smile. "I have your attention now, don't I? Where is it?"

I have to force air in and out of my lungs. Emotions swirl inside me, too tangled for me to even sort them out.

How does she know about it? It's not possible. The police have no clues in the murder, and I never said a word about that night. That book is a piece of my old life—the one I can't bear to think about anymore.

"Maybe you do want to get out of here, but you're afraid," Dr. Heaton says, her tone cool and collected. "So let me help. Tell me where it is."

I swallow hard, dizzy even though I'm sitting down. Realization is hitting like a punch I never saw coming.

If she can't know about it, and I'm sitting here with her right now and she *does* know about it, is this really happening? Am I like Leonard, trapped in a reality that only I can see?

I start to breathe hard, my chest tightening as the room spins faster. Holy shit. All this time, I've been telling myself I don't belong here, but what if I do? What if that night I had a complete break with reality?

Dr. Heaton is talking, but I can't hear her. There's a whooshing sound in my ears as I get up from the couch and walk toward the door, my arms out in front of me in case I fall.

The CNA in the hallway rushes toward me when I walk out of the room.

"Allison, what is it? Are you okay?"

I turn to her, my vision blurred by tears.

"Do you want to go to your room?"

When I don't respond, she takes me by the elbow and leads me away. Dr. Heaton comes out of her office and exchanges a few words with the CNA, but I can't hear them. I can't process anything right now.

I want Daniel. I want his arms around me, and I don't care who sees.

But . . . wait. Does he know I'm delusional? He must—he's a doctor, after all. Suddenly, I'm filled with shame. For all I know, I made up his attraction to me.

Helplessness surrounds me. There's a big part of me that wants Daniel no matter what. Even if he is just my doctor, he's also my comfort. He's the one person I trust completely.

I look around for him as the CNA leads me back to my room. My heart sinks when I remember he's off this week because his son is here. If I ask for a doctor, I'll get Dr. Tillman. That's not happening.

We pass Morgan, and she smiles brightly at me. "Hey, do you want to—" She stops talking when she meets my eyes. "What's wrong?"

"I think she just needs a rest," the CNA says, patting my arm. "Give her a couple hours to herself."

Morgan nods and I'm led into my room, where I lie down on the bed, too numb to care that my shoes are still on. The CNA covers me up with a blanket and pulls the blinds closed.

I can't sleep. I just stare at the wall and take inventory, trying to figure out what's real and what's not. I suppose the first step is to consider what's real *to me*. And then, like Leonard, I may need to be told some hard truths.

Chapter
SIXTEEN

WATCHING CALEB WALK away with his mom at the airport leaves me feeling empty. Our week together was great, but it passed too quickly.

He turns around when he's about ten feet away and runs back to give me one last hug. It's all I can do not to break down as he squeezes me with his little arms.

"Love you, Dad," he says, giving me a gap-toothed grin.

"Love you, too. I'll see you in September."

He nods and walks back to Julie, who meets my eyes with a grateful smile. I wave and watch them walk away until Caleb is out of sight, and then head back to the airline desk to check in for my flight back to Montana.

The airline would have let him fly alone, but I wasn't comfortable with that, and neither was Julie, so I flew to LA to get him and then flew back with him after our time together. Having him visit me at Hawthorne meant more than I can put into words. He got to see what I do and where I live and explore the woods I've come to love.

In September, I'm flying to LA to spend three days with him at a hotel. And even though that feels like a long way off, and even though I know I'll miss him like crazy when I get home and see the box of Lucky Charms on my kitchen table, I feel good.

This is a start. Julie trusts that I'm staying sober and is giving me another chance with Caleb, which is more than I deserve. He has a stepdad now, and she could easily just write me off and I'd have no grounds to complain.

I'm already planning a long camping trip when Caleb comes back next summer. He loved the two nights we spent tent camping. I was relieved because I'd wondered if my big-city son would still appreciate the outdoors like I do.

On the flight back to Helena, my thoughts are a mix of my son and Hawthorne. Tillman held down the fort while I was gone, but there's a lot of paperwork to catch up on.

And then there's Allison. The past couple nights when I've caught glimpses of her at dinner, she's had dark circles under her eyes and looked almost vacant. Something's not right with her, and I'm anxious to find her as soon as I get back and find out what's going on.

I had to fight my instinct to go to her as soon as I noticed something was off. I'd promised myself that the week Caleb was here, he'd have my full attention and Tillman would be responsible for patient care.

Allison's more than just a patient to me, though. I can't stand to see her upset. All I can do is think about what might have happened on the long flight and then the long drive back to Hawthorne.

Did seeing me with Caleb bother her somehow? I doubt it. She already knew about him.

Could she have gotten bad news about a family member? From her patient file, I know she doesn't have anyone left but an aunt in New York. Damn, I hope nothing happened to her only relative.

That's a possibility, but my money's on Heaton. I've only seen Allison upset one other time, and it was because of Heaton. I told the Hawthorne administration I'm concerned about how Heaton is treating patients, but nothing's come of it yet.

By the time I get back to Hawthorne, it's late. I'm restless, so I go to my office to catch up on paperwork. When I switch on the lights, I see that the last book I gave Allison, *The Road*, is sitting on the corner of my desk.

I grab it and flip open the cover, hoping to see a note from her that will assure me she's okay.

There's nothing. I flip through all the pages and shake the book, hoping a slip of paper will fall out, but the book is empty.

Fuck, now I'm really worried. She's never returned a book without leaving me a note.

I go through all my patient reports from Tillman, wondering if he's noticed something off with Allison. If he has, he didn't include it in his reports.

With a heavy sigh, I run my hand down my face. It's not like I can go upstairs and wake her up. I'll have to wait until tomorrow.

I get out my tablet and go through new emails. Time gets away from me, and it's after three in the morning by the time I turn off the lamp and lie down on the leather couch in my office. I've spent many a night sleeping here, and it doesn't take me long to drift off.

The next morning, I'm woken up by a hand on my arm and warm breath on my cheek.

"Dr. D, hey. Wake up."

I open my eyes and flinch when I see Sara, her face just inches from mine.

"Relax, it's just me," she says, smiling and squeezing my bicep. She's got a fascination with that part of me for some reason.

"Hey." I sit up and squint, trying to make out the time on my wall clock.

"It's eight," she says. "Time for rounds. And can I just tell you how adorable Caleb is? He's handsome like his daddy."

"Thanks." I get up from the couch. "I'll be out for rounds in five minutes."

She leaves my office and I walk into my bathroom. I change into a clean T-shirt and brush my teeth. I keep essentials in this bathroom for nights I sleep in my office. Turning my face to one side and then the other in the mirror, I consider shaving. I've got a full coating of dark stubble.

Nah. I'll shave tomorrow.

Taking my white coat from a hook on the wall, I head for the staff lounge, putting it on as I walk.

I ignore the morning chatter from the staff as I pour myself a cup of coffee. I'm not in the mood for chatter. Not that I ever am, but especially not today.

Tillman's off, so I have to round on all the patients myself. He kept things running smoothly in my absence, so it goes as quickly as it can. Billy McGrath's current personality has a thick Irish brogue, and it takes me a while to understand what he's saying. It's nothing important, but I shoot the shit with him for a few minutes anyway.

By the time I get to Allison's room, I feel like a caged beast. I need to know what's going on with her, and I can't wait another minute.

When I open the door and walk in, I see her curled up on top of her bed, the sun shining on her dark hair.

Some of my tension fades. She looks peaceful and relaxed, and I know she needs the rest. I close her door and go back to the staff lounge for more coffee, then into my office.

By the scents of roast beef and garlic I'm picking up, I know it's close to lunchtime. My stomach rumbles its approval of the menu as I upload notes from my tablet on to my computer. All in all, things are good here. Leonard is doing better.

Now if I can just figure out what's up with Allison.

There's a soft knock on my door and someone slowly opens it. When I see Allison's face, my shoulders sink with relief. I get up from my desk chair and walk around to meet her.

She's still standing in the doorway when I get there, a tentative look in her eyes. There are still dark shadows beneath her eyes, and my concern grows stronger than before.

"Hey," I say softly. "Come in."

She steps inside, and I close the door behind her. Before I can stop myself, I'm wrapping her in my arms, holding her as close as I've been wanting to for the past few weeks.

She relaxes against me, her cheek on my chest.

"I'm worried about you," I murmur against her hair. "Are you okay?"

She nods, her arms encircling my back. I pull back from her and cup her face in my hands, studying her expression.

By the tears in her eyes, I know she's anything but okay.

"What is it?" I ask her.

She tips her face up toward me and looks at me through her long, dark lashes. I forget everything else, leaning down to kiss her. She makes a soft moaning sound that sets me off, and I reach down and cup her ass, picking her up.

She's giving me the same passion in return, her tongue sliding against mine as she wraps her legs around me. I walk her over to my desk and set her on it, my pent-up desire for her almost too much to hold back.

I want to rip her clothes off and bury myself inside her. Whatever's upsetting her, I want to take it away. I've only had a small taste of her, and it's not enough. I want to taste every inch of her, hear her say my name, feel her contract around me as she comes.

"I've missed you," I say against her mouth, my hands locked around her tiny waist.

I lean my forehead against hers, and we breathe in unison for a few seconds, both of us drawing each other in as much as the air around us.

Allison breaks away from me and reaches for a piece of paper on my desk. She picks up a pen and writes out a message.

I think I might be delusional. Like Leonard.

Her brow is furrowed with worry. I stroke a hand over her hair. "Why do you think that?"
She writes on the paper again.

Don't lie to me. Tell me if you think I might be losing my mind. Please.

Her eyes are wide and frantic. I kiss her gently. It pains me that she's been dealing with this worry all alone.

"I don't think you're losing your mind, Allison. I truly don't. Tell me what's got you so worried about this."

She closes her eyes and looks down. I put my thumb under her chin and lift it until her eyes meet mine.

"Tell me. You know it's safe with me, whatever it is."

Turning back to the paper on the desk, she writes some more.

Dr. Heaton knows something, and I don't know how she knows it. Something I didn't tell her. How could she know?

"Something about that night?"
She nods, her expression mournful.

"I know she's talked to the detectives investigating the case. Could it be something they told her?"

She considers this for a second, then shakes her head. She

shrugs after that, and I can tell she's unsure. Not to mention frustrated as hell and probably exhausted.

"Listen. I'll talk to her about it. And if I don't get the answers, I'll call the Chicago PD myself and ask. We'll figure this out, okay? Don't—"

There's a knock on my office door, and Allison jumps.

"Dr. Delgado, it's lunchtime," Sara says through the door. "I'll save you a seat."

"That's okay, I'll grab something in a bit."

I step away from my desk, and Allison slides down from the edge. Sara could open the door, and it wouldn't be good for her to see us like this.

She walks away, though, and I give Allison a reassuring look. "Hey. You're okay. We'll figure this out. And you can stop going to the sessions with Heaton if they're bothering you."

With a slight smile, she takes my big hand in her two small ones and brings it to her lips, kissing the back of it. The brush of her soft lips across my skin sends a hot flare of need for her down my spine.

"Someday," I say in a low tone. "In another time and place, Allison. I promise you, someday we'll have more than this."

She puts my palm on her cheek, and I brush my thumb over her cheekbone. Whatever it takes, I'll keep that promise, which I wasn't only making to her, but also to myself.

Chapter
SEVENTEEN

THAT DAY, I find some peace again, Daniel's words still replaying in my mind. He doesn't think I'm crazy. He said *we'll* figure this out. Not *him*, or *me*, but *we*—me and him. Just telling him what I'm feeling and not being alone anymore is a weight off my shoulders.

"Hey." Morgan walks into my room and does a full spin. "Do these pajamas say casual chic? I want to look good without looking like I'm trying to look good."

I look over her light gray top and black shorts and give her a thumbs-up. She grins and leaves the room as fast as she came in.

Since Milo got here, I don't see much of Morgan anymore. They spend most of their free time together. I miss her more than I thought I would. There's something about Morgan and her non-stop one-sided conversations about this place that makes me feel normal. It's too quiet without her keeping me company.

I open my book, *Little Women*, and can't even finish a whole chapter before my eyes are closing on their own. It's been several days since I've had a good night of sleep. Now that I'm feeling better, I hope to catch up tonight.

The dream finds me, though.

"Who killed Ava? They know you know, Allison. Just tell me. Tell me, and I'll let you rest."

I murmur something, answering the man before my mind can process what he's saying. Then I squeeze my mouth shut. I can't tell him anything. I can't tell anyone.

"It's okay. You can tell me."

I fight back against the heavy, foggy cloud of the dream. I won't talk—not even in a dream.

A stinging sensation makes me lurch, my eyes flying open. The room is dark, but I can make out a figure next to me. I scream, not getting much out before I need to suck in another breath.

A cloth is pressed over my mouth, and I bring my hands up to fight against suffocation. I want to scream for Daniel, but I can't make a sound. Within a few seconds, my muscles go slack and I'm drifting back into the darkness.

I wake up to the dark room, inhaling sharply as I look next to my bed for the figure I saw earlier. Of course, there's no one there. It was just a dream.

My stomach is churning and my heart is hammering as I sit up in bed. *Was* it just a dream? It felt so real. I touch my face, still feeling tender from the cloth that was pressed over my mouth. And the stinging sensation in my arm—I still feel it.

I pull my legs up to my chest, terror making it hard to even breathe. Something is very wrong. That voice. That deep, unfamiliar voice that's been asking for answers all these months. What if it was real all along?

I want Daniel. I want to run to his cabin right now and crawl into his bed. I'm shaking, filled with the same terror I felt that night.

"They know you know." That's what the man said.

How does he know who they are? It has to mean they know I'm here. It has to mean they sent him.

And that means my life is in danger. Silent tears slide down my cheeks as I realize that Hawthorne Hill, my safe place, isn't safe anymore.

I can't go back to sleep. I can't even lie down. I just sit in my bed, my legs pulled up to my chest and my arms wrapped around my legs, waiting. If the man comes back, I won't be asleep next time. Soon the dim light of day starts filtering into my room.

There's no escaping it. Even in the Montana woods, as far removed from downtown Chicago as I could be, there's no out-running it. I've been crying for hours by the time I hear footsteps in the hallway.

I slide out of bed and dress in jeans and a T-shirt, my hands shaking. Once I've put on my ballet flats, I leave my room, looking both ways down the hallway when I open the door. I can't be sure of anything now. Whoever that man is, he could find me here at any moment. He could do much worse than that.

I hurry downstairs to Daniel's office, sitting in the hallway against the wall until he walks in through a side entrance. He's freshly shaved, wearing a pale blue polo shirt with a leather messenger bag slung over his shoulder.

"Hey," he says when he sees me, lowering his brows with worry.

I stand up and put my hand on the doorknob. He gets the message, putting a key in the lock and turning it to open the door.

Once we're both inside and he's closed the door behind us, I let the tears come. He wraps his arms around me as I cry harder than I have since that night. My chest is heaving with sobs, and I just can't make myself stop.

"You're okay," Daniel says, holding me close as I come undone. "I've got you."

It's time. I may not be ready, and I may be terrified, but it's time to push myself forward anyway.

"Daniel," I say softly.

He pulls back, eyes full of wonder as he looks at me.

"I need your help," I say, my unused voice barely a whisper.

"Of course. Anything."

He leads me over to his dark brown leather couch, where we both sit down and he wraps his arm around me.

I take a deep breath and look at him. "I'm in trouble. There are people who want to find me and . . . they probably want to kill me, too."

"They can't find you here." He rubs my shoulder reassuringly. "You're safe here."

"I'm not, though." I force down the lump in my throat. "I've been having this dream—this horrible dream, pretty much since I got here. That a man is trying to make me tell him what I know about that night. Only last night I woke up, and it wasn't a dream. Daniel, it wasn't. I know it."

His palm is on my back now, making reassuring strokes up and down. "Okay. Let's talk this through."

I put my elbows on my knees and bury my face in my hands. "You don't believe me. And I can't say I blame you since this is a mental hospital and I'm a patient here."

My soft laugh is anything but amused. Daniel hands me a tissue from a side table, and I wipe my nose.

"Hey. I believe you, okay? I do."

I look over at him, shaking my head. "But how can you? I don't even know if I believe myself. I just know that last night . . . it felt so real, and there was a man with a cloth over my mouth and a stinging in my arm."

He turns his body to face mine. "What kind of stinging? Where?"

I put my fingers on the sore spot, and he gets up and walks over to his desk.

"Can you come over here?" he says.

When I move to stand behind his desk with him, he pulls the blinds all the way up and puts on his reading glasses. He leans down and examines the spot on my arm, his brow wrinkled with disapproval.

"I see something. It looks like a needle mark."

I pull my arm back with disbelief. "A needle mark?"

He nods, looking grim.

"Can you close the blinds?" I ask, my eyes filling with tears again.

Daniel and I stand behind his desk, facing each other. There was a small part of me that hoped this was all in my mind, maybe brought on by post-traumatic stress disorder. It's real, though. Painfully real.

He puts his hands on my upper arms, rubbing them. "You need to tell me everything, Allison. I haven't wanted to push you, but if you're in danger, I need to know everything so I can help you."

I nod, swallowing hard. "The people who are after me are from Chicago. They're the ones who killed my sister."

"But they didn't kill you that night, so why do they want to now?"

"I was strangled. They tried to kill me. My neighbor yelled through the door that he'd called the police, and they left."

"Do you know who they are?"

"Yeah, I know who they are," I whisper, looking down at my feet.

"And that's why they want you dead? Because you can identify them as the people who killed Ava?"

"Either that, or they've figured out the truth." My voice shakes as I finally admit it. "Which is that I *am* Ava."

Chapter
EIGHTEEN

March 16, 2016

MY APARTMENT'S SOUND system is playing a soulful song by Adele. I've got one of her albums on, because I'm just in an Adele kind of mood.

The tray of baked ziti I ordered from my favorite Italian place is staying warm in the oven. I'm also in a pasta kind of mood, but I'm waiting for my sister to get here so we can eat together.

A knock sounds on my door, and I get up from my couch to answer it, bringing my glass of white wine with me.

"Hey," Allison says from the other side of the door.

"Hi."

She smiles, and I step aside so she can come in. And just like that, my mood is lifted. She's always had that effect on me.

I close the door, and she sets down the bag she's carrying. When I turn to face her, she reaches out to me, hugging me tight.

"I'm sorry," she says softly. "I really am."

My throat tightens as I hug her back with one arm, keeping ahold of my wineglass with my other hand. "Thanks."

She pulls back and squeezes my upper arms gently, brushing a lock of hair from my face. "Better to find out the truth now than after you married him, right?"

I nod, because she's right. I should have listened to her suspicions about my fiancé. Of the two of us, Allison has always been the practical one. The look before you leap one. I'm impulsive, and at times, reckless. And that's how I got into this shitty situation that requires Adele, cheesy pasta, lots of wine, and a reconciliation with my twin sister, whom I never should have been mad at to begin with.

We've been mirror images of each other since the day we were born. Same height, same long dark hair, same big brown eyes. And even though our personalities are different, we have common ground. We both love cheesy comedies and Little Debbie snack cakes. We agree that expensive wine is often overrated. And we're fiercely devoted to each other.

Allison picks up the bag she brought and pulls out a bottle of white wine.

"There's already a bottle open in the kitchen," I tell her.

"I'll throw this one in the fridge, then."

She walks into the kitchen and inhales deeply. "Giordano's ziti?"

"You know it. And breadsticks with all the cheese dips. And cinnamon bread. This is an occasion for all the carbs."

My sister gives me a sympathetic look. "I'm sorry, Ava."

"I just wish I would have listened to you to begin with. But Dax . . ."

"He's very charming," she says. "And attractive. Well-off. Any woman would be flattered by his attention."

I snort-laugh and take a sip of my wine. "Yeah, he's well-off because of killing his competition to corner the market on drug dealing."

Allison inhales sharply. "I didn't realize he was *that* bad."

I sit down across from her at the small kitchen table in my downtown loft. "You've been telling me since the first time you met him that you had a bad feeling. I thought it was just . . . I don't know."

"Me being jealous?" She smiles and grabs my glass, taking a sip of the wine.

"Not jealous so much as possessive. Things moved fast with me and Dax. We got engaged after seven months of dating."

She looks down at the round, vibrant blue diamond on my left hand. "So did you confront him about what he does for a living?"

I sigh heavily. "No, but I'll have to. He has this black, leather-bound notebook that he carries everywhere. He's fanatical about it. Says he doesn't trust computers because they can be hacked, so the notebook has all his important business information in it."

Allison's face pales. "Oh, no. Tell me you didn't take it."

"What else could I do? I had to know, so I took it from his apartment this morning while he was still asleep. I had this nagging sense that you were right. I *missed* you. We haven't really talked in more than a month. I just wanted to know, once and for all, so I could either tell you that you were wrong or . . ."

She reaches for my hand. "You hadn't really considered the or, had you?"

I shake my head miserably. "Dax is intense, but I never thought he was . . . a bad person, you know? He's been so good to me."

"So you're sure what you saw in the notebook proves what you're thinking?"

"I'm sure. I Googled some of the names and dates, and there were news stories about murders. And also . . ." I clear my throat, trying to force away the lump lodged there.

"What is it?"

"Women. Photos and phone numbers with . . ." I shake my head in disgust. "Notes about what they do best in bed."

"Oh, fuck him."

"Yeah."

Allison looks around my kitchen. "Where's the notebook now? Did you just look at it, or did you take it?"

"I've got it. I needed time to go through it."

"Ava." Her eyes are wide with worry. "Dax isn't going to like this."

"Well, I don't like being lied to and cheated on."

She gives me an exasperated look. "You need to get out of town, and I'm not kidding. Mail that notebook back to him and go lie low at the beach house."

"I've got work to do."

"You think Dax Caldwell will let you just hand him that notebook and your engagement ring and walk away?" Her voice is laced with anger now.

"I'll handle him."

I slip off the ring and admire it. "It was too good to be true, I guess. When he gave me this ring, I felt like the luckiest woman in the world."

"It's beautiful. Maybe you should keep it."

I set it on the table. "I don't even want it. That asshole can save it for his next fiancée."

Allison picks up the ring and slides it on her finger. "Wow. This thing had to cost at least a hundred grand."

"Blood money," I say bitterly.

There's a knock at my door, and I get up to answer it. Two men in dark coats give me tight smiles.

"Delivery for Miss Cole," the stockier one says.

"Oh." I'm not expecting anything, and my first thought is that it's a gift from Dax, which I don't want.

"It's heavy," he says, gesturing to the box in the other man's hands. "We'll just bring it in for you."

He pushes past me, the other man following him in and closing the door.

"Wait, what is it?" I put up a hand as he starts opening the box.

He takes out rope and a handgun, pointing the weapon right at me. I'm stunned for a second, but then I scream, blood rushing to my head.

"What's going on?" Allison rushes into the room, and as soon as she sees the gun, she screams, too.

"There's two of 'em?" the tall man says to the stocky one. "What the fuck?"

"I don't fuckin' know. Grab that one."

The stocky man reaches for me, and I back up a few steps to stay out of his reach. "My purse is in the kitchen," I say, my voice shaking. "Take anything you want."

"This ain't a robbery." He grabs my arm and drags me toward the kitchen.

I have to fight. I'm not about to give in to whatever these guys have planned. I dig in my feet, scream, kick, and claw. From what I can hear, Allison is doing the same to the other man.

The man pulls something out of his coat pocket and ties it around my mouth, tossing another one to his friend. Allison's screams quiet as she's gagged, too.

A new wave of terror sweeps through me as my wrists are squeezed behind my back and I'm shoved down to my knees. My eyes meet Allison's, and I see the same fear in hers.

"I'm not doin' two," the taller man says. "Caldwell only paid us for one."

What does he mean? What the hell does he mean? An inner voice is screaming in my head. Caldwell. So Dax—my fiancé—sent these two men here. I hope to God he just sent them here to get me. If he knows I took the book, I'll return it and beg for mercy.

The stocky guy looks in the box he left on the floor. "Where's the silencer?"

Silencer? I nearly pee my pants, and I start screaming again, the sound muffled by the gag.

"I thought you had it," the taller one says.

He glares. "I told you to bring it, dumbass."

There's a sharp knock on my door.

"Ava? Are you okay?"

I recognize the voice of my neighbor, Jeff. Tears fill my eyes as I scream against the fabric over my mouth.

He knocks again. "Ava? I thought I heard screaming."

Hope surges through my chest. The two men exchange looks.

"What the fuck are we gonna do?" the tall one hisses in a whisper.

"Improvise." The stocky one grabs my hair and whips my head back, making me cry out in pain.

"Which one of you is Ava Cole?" he growls at me.

I'm screaming against the gag, trying to tell him it's me, my heart pounding against my rib cage as I realize what's about to happen.

"We have to do both of 'em, don't we?" the tall one mutters. "Caldwell better pay for the other one."

His partner gives him a pissed-off scowl. "We'll tell him the job's done and that's it, you stupid shit. You ever want to work for him again, you don't bother him with the details. Now will you hurry the fuck up and do it? The neighbor could come back."

He puts his face just a couple inches from mine. "Which one of you is Ava?"

His teeth are yellow, and his brown beard is patchy. Tears fall from my eyes as I nod and frantically tell him it's me. He still has my hands pinned behind my back, so I can't do much else.

When I look over at Allison, I see the other man tying her hands up with rope. She's so scared. I can see it and feel it. I'm scared, too. This is all my fault. I should have listened when I first started seeing Dax and she told me she had a bad feeling about him. Or just walked away instead of taking his book.

The other man walks into the kitchen and returns with a butcher knife from the block on my counter. I scream and thrash against the man holding me. He pushes my head, and I hit the ground, his knee coming down on my back.

The tall one has the knife in front of Allison's throat now. I'm sobbing, struggling to breathe through the gag. This is a nightmare. My sister's life is hanging by a thread, all because I was stupid and selfish.

"Which one of you is Ava?" the tall one asks again. He grabs my hair and pulls hard. I see small dots of light in my vision.

Allison is squirming and turning her body around. She's moving her hands. The tall man looks closer at them, then unties them. She holds a hand up in front of her, and I almost stop breathing.

"It's her," he says. "She's got the big fuckin' rock Caldwell bought her."

No. The word is coursing through my body. No, please, no. She's lying to them in hopes of saving me. I don't want this. I can't live a life without her.

The tall man grabs her hair, pulls her head back, and runs the knife across her throat in one smooth motion. A bright red line appears on my sister's neck, and I scream as blood starts spilling from it.

She drops to the floor, her eyes finding mine. I crawl to her, never looking away. There's peace in her soft brown eyes, and love, even now, as her life is draining away.

My throat burns from screaming. My bladder empties, probably out of sheer terror. Nothing these men can do now will scare me. They've taken away the other half of my heart.

I tell her I love her and it's going to be okay, though my words are too muffled for her to understand. And just as I see the light leave her eyes, my throat tightens as hands close around it.

"This is cleaner, dumbass," he says to the other man as he squeezes my throat. "No DNA."

I don't look away from Allison. I want her to be the last thing I see. The red of the blood pooling on the floor next to her starts to swirl in with colors around it as my vision blurs.

A knock sounds on the door. "Ava, the police are on their way. If you're inside, open up."

The pressure on my throat lets up, and I hear the men running down the hall toward my bedroom.

"Out the window," I hear one of them say. "Hurry the fuck up."

My lungs want to drag in as much air as possible, but the gag won't allow it. I want to hold Allison, but my hands are still bound. I feel dizzy.

I don't know if seconds or minutes pass, but soon my door is being broken down, and two uniformed police officers come inside.

A female officer drops down to the floor and pulls the gag away from my mouth.

"Are you okay?" she asks.

I open my mouth to speak but then close it again. What is there to say? I'm not okay, and I never will be again. I just wish that hitman had pushed on my windpipe a little harder, choked a little longer. Allison is dead because of me, and I'd give anything to trade places with her.

Chapter
NINETEEN

I'M STUNNED INTO silence for a couple seconds. Ava's revelation left me reeling. Her wide eyes are pleading with me to say something.

"I'm sorry."

The words are barely out of my mouth before she reaches for both of my hands, holding on to them as she looks at me. "Please believe me, Daniel. I need you to believe me."

"I believe you."

Tears pool in her eyes. "I've been thinking about this conversation for hours, and I came up with so many reasons for you not to believe me. I was afraid you'd think I'm delusional."

"No." I bring one of her hands to my mouth and kiss her knuckles. "You've given me no reason to think that."

She smiles and tears spill past her lower eyelashes. "You mean, other than the fact that you're treating me at a mental hospital?"

A corner of my mouth turns up in a smile. "Now I know why you're here, though. And I can't say I blame you for staying silent."

She sighs softly and looks away. "It wasn't about protecting myself. Not at first. I was just so shattered . . ." Her voice wavers with emotion. "There was nothing worth saying anymore. Nothing worth doing. It's why I kept ripping out my IV lines when I got here. I just wanted to be free from the pain."

I take a deep breath, still processing everything she just told me. "How did no one catch this? The coroner or . . . I don't know, *someone.*"

"Because she was wearing the engagement ring, there was never a question. My aunt Maggie identified her, so there was no need to look at dental records or anything."

"So there was a funeral . . . for you?"

She shrugs. "There was, but I didn't go. I guess my business partner took care of the arrangements, but Aunt Maggie didn't think I was stable enough to go. She was probably right. I was in shock for a long time, and when the grief hit . . ." She shakes her head, her voice tight with emotion. "It hit like a tidal wave."

Cupping her cheeks, I raise her face so I can look into her eyes. "You're the one who was engaged. The one with the design business. This whole time, I thought . . ."

"That I was the nice one?"

"No. I just . . . it's a lot to process."

"I haven't faked anything with you, Daniel. The only thing you didn't know about me was my real name."

I shake my head. "I didn't know you were engaged to some asshole drug lord who tried to have you killed over a book. Or that you're actually a millionaire business owner."

"Not anymore. I haven't thought about Brighton Cole at all since that night."

"Brighton Cole?"

"The fashion label I co-own with my business partner, Madeline. Or . . . co-*owned* . . . I guess. I don't care about any of that anymore. My stupid, selfish drive to be successful is what got Allie killed."

"How so?" I slide a hand around to the back of her neck and

rub it gently.

"I ignored the signs about Dax because he was powerful. He was smooth and confident, and I wanted to be part of his world."

Her brow is furrowed, and her eyes are swimming with pain and guilt. I can't help pulling her close to me.

"Hey. You couldn't have known he'd do this."

She shakes her head. "I knew he was capable. As soon as I saw in that book that he'd had people killed, I should have gone to the police. If I had, my sister would still be alive."

Pressing her face to my chest, she breaks down in tears. It's the first time I've seen her give in to her sadness. She needs this.

"You still have the book?" I whisper, my cheek resting on her silky hair.

After a moment's hesitation, she says, "It's hidden. In Chicago."

I take a few seconds to process things. It was enough of a shock to find out it's not Allison Cole I'm falling for, as I thought, but Ava. And she's in danger. She also just spoke, and the first word she said was my name.

I'm a problem solver. It's a skill I learned in the military that still serves me well as a doctor. In life-or-death situations, I isolate the problem and create steps to solve it.

"We need to find out who came into your room," I say, talking to myself as much as Ava. "If I go to the Hawthorne administration with this, we might not find out who it was for sure. They'll start questioning the staff, and word will get out."

"Is there any chance I imagined it?" She looks up at me. "I've been having dreams about him for months. I just can't even . . . Has it been a real person all along? And what have I told him?"

She looks like she might be sick, and from the dark circles under her eyes, I know she's exhausted.

"If you'd told him what he wanted to know, he wouldn't keep coming back," I tell her. "And from the needle mark on your arm,

I don't think there's any chance you imagined it."

She sighs heavily.

"Here's what we're gonna do," I say. "I want you to ask Morgan to sit in your room with you for a few hours. I'll give you something to help you sleep. And trust me to figure something out to catch the guy who came into your room."

"Don't tell Dr. Heaton."

I narrow my eyes. "Is she bothering you again?"

"I just have a bad feeling about her, Daniel. She asked me about the book, and there's no way she should have known about it. Unless the police know about it. Maybe Dax figured out it wasn't me they killed. I don't know."

"Have I told you about my army buddy, Sam?"

She scrunches her forehead in confusion. "No."

"We served in combat together. There's no bond like that. And now he's a detective for the Chicago Police Department."

There's a flicker of hope in her eyes.

"Do you trust me?" I ask her.

"Yes."

"Then rest while I figure some things out. And don't tell anyone else any of this."

She nods. "I don't feel like talking to anyone else, anyway."

I wrap my arms around her, and she presses herself against my chest. It feels good. Ava's trust in me makes me want her even more than I did before.

There's a knock on my door, and Ava jumps out of my arms. I put a finger to my lips so she knows to stay quiet, and then I walk over to the door and crack it open so whoever it is can't see her.

"Morning," Sara says with a smile. "Did you forget the staff meeting?"

"Oh, shit. I did."

She waits a couple seconds, then gives me an expectant look.

"Well, let's go."

"I'll be there in a few minutes. Just have to take care of something first."

"We can't start without you."

I hold back the impatient glare I want to give her. "Sure, you can. You guys know the drill."

She shrugs. "Okay. See you in a little bit."

I close the door and turn back to Ava. She's standing with her arms crossed, looking a little more settled than she did earlier.

"What are the stages of grief?" Her tone is quiet and controlled.

"Uh . . . let's see. Denial, anger . . . bargaining, depression, and then acceptance."

She nods. "I guess I've been in denial this whole time. It just hurt too much to really accept living without her. But now . . . God, it happened so quickly. Now I'm angry. So fucking angry. I want to kill Dax and those two men he sent to my apartment. I want them to feel what she did." Her voice breaks and tears flood her eyes.

"I understand. But one thing at a time, okay? I'm going to get some medication for you from the supply room. Meet me up in your room."

When she walks toward me, in the direction of the door, I'm drawn to her in a way I can't resist. I wrap my arms around her again and pull her against me, lifting her feet from the floor. She cups my cheeks and kisses me softly.

"Thank you," she says against my lips. "For helping me and believing me. For everything."

"I won't let anything happen to you." I set her feet back on the floor and take a deep breath to compose myself before I open my office door and we walk out.

Alli—I mean, Ava—puts her head down and makes her way down the hallway, toward the great room and the main staircase.

I'm right behind her, on my way to the medical supply room, when I see Sara standing at the end of the hallway looking at me.

For once, she's not giving me a flirtatious smile. It's more like a glare.

Fuck. She saw Ava come out of my office.

AFTER I GIVE Ava some medication to help her sleep and leave her in Morgan's care in her room, I step in for the second half of the staff meeting. It's all perfunctory stuff, and my mind keeps wandering to Ava.

If someone is able to get into Hawthorne without authorization, in the middle of the night, no less, we have serious security issues. That concerns me, especially knowing how crucial security is for our Level Three patients. There are psychopaths up there who would feel no remorse over the crimes they could commit if they got out.

I pull Tillman aside after the meeting. "Hey, will you be okay without me for a couple hours?"

"Yeah. Everything okay?"

"I just need to go into town for a little while. I'll be back by this afternoon."

He starts morning rounds, and I go get the keys to one of the SUVs owned by Hawthorne. The dark Expedition doesn't get much use because Joanne Hawthorne bought it for my use when she hired me, and I'm careful not to leave here unless I have to. Just because I don't go out searching for the temptation of alcohol, that doesn't mean it wouldn't find me.

I normally don't feel an urge to drink anymore, but the old craving is creeping in today. As soon as I'm away from the safety of Hawthorne, where there's no alcohol, my body seems to react physically.

The town of Greenville is only about twenty minutes away,

and I decide to call Sam on the car's Bluetooth to get my mind off drinking. I push the button on my cell phone, and it connects to the Expedition's speakers.

"Delgado," he says when he answers. "How the hell are you?"

I smile at the enthusiasm in his deep voice. "I'm good, man. How about you?"

"Not bad. Busy with work. Where are you these days, still in Montana?"

"Yeah."

"You like it there?"

"I do. You should come up and go hunting with me this fall."

"Say no more. I'm in."

I clear my throat. "I'm actually not calling just to talk."

"Yeah, no shit. You never do. That's why I haven't talked to you in a year. What's up?"

I tell him about the open murder case, leaving out the part about it being Allison and not Ava who was actually murdered.

"Doesn't ring a bell, but I'll look it up," he says. "I'm doing gang enforcement these days."

"Kicking some ass?"

He laughs. "Something like that."

"I need to know as much as you can get me on that case. As soon as possible."

"You got it, brother." He pauses. "Hey, you still clean and sober?"

"Two years sober. I was never on drugs, dumbass."

"Good thing, since you've got a supply on hand. Don't fucking go there, man. You've got a good thing going up there; I can tell by your voice."

I nod. "Yeah. You're right."

"Okay, I'll do some checking on this case and call you back."

"Thanks, Sam."

"Anytime."

I push the button on the Expedition's dash to end the call, sighing deeply. He's right. I've come a long way in the past two years. Ava's counting on me. And Caleb . . . I smile as I think about his recent visit.

This is my second chance, and I'm not letting the people I care about down. I drive past a liquor store and two bars in Greenville. Even though they aren't open yet, I know I could handle the temptation if they were.

My destination is a small gun shop downtown. I've bought shotguns here, and I know the owner, Pike, will have what I need. He's one of those guys who has everything.

I park and walk into the tobacco-scented storefront with purpose. Ava's not the only one who's angry. Whoever assaulted her last night is never getting away with it again.

Chapter
TWENTY

I JUST CAN'T relax. It's the third night since I told Daniel what happened, and I'm wondering if this will be the night the man comes back to prod me for answers.

Or will it be another night of quiet, with me just pretending to sleep as I wait for someone to show up but no one ever does? Another night where I wonder whether the man is only a figment of my traumatized mind.

After a drink of water, I return to my position curled up on my side with my eyes closed. It looks like I'm asleep, but it's after 2:00 a.m. and I haven't slept yet tonight. I'm tired enough, but the worry about what might happen if I drift off keeps me awake.

If the man who injected me returns, Daniel will know. We're actually hoping he'll return so we can get some answers. And if he does, the tiny camera Daniel installed across from my bed will alert him. He set it up so the camera kicks on at 9:00 p.m., and any movement sends an alert to his cell phone. That drink of water I just had may have woken him up.

He's sleeping on the couch in his office, though from the

shadows under his eyes, I don't think he's sleeping much more than me. I'm so lucky to have him in my corner.

For so long after Allison died, all I heard in my mind were the unending screams of my own grief. I was emotionally paralyzed, unable to imagine feeling anything but despair and hopelessness ever again.

I'm feeling more now, though. Daniel sparked a tiny flame inside me that took a long time to grow into something sure. Something that won't be snuffed out by the slightest breeze.

Anger, desire, frustration, gratitude. I never thought there would be room for those feelings in my shattered heart again. He made room, though. Or maybe he made me want to clear the way myself. Either way, I'm alive again. It's bittersweet, because it means I'm healing from Allison's death, however slowly.

I don't deserve that. It should be me in that dark wood casket buried beneath the headstone marked with my name. She took my place and died the death that was meant for me.

I'm replaying my final conversation with her, trying to recall every expression on her face and every word she said, when I feel myself being pulled into a twilight state. I'm fighting to stay awake, but it's a losing battle.

Movement wakes me up. I'm in a fog, my movements slower as I open my eyes and try to focus in the darkness.

A big, dark form is practically flying across the room.

"You better be scared," he says in a low growl.

Daniel.

He pulls another figure away from my bedside, slamming them against the wall. From the groan of pain, I can tell it's a man.

The man who's been asking me questions while I sleep. It was real. I feel a sense of relief and apprehension at the same time.

"What the fuck do you think you're doing?" Daniel has the man pressed against the wall, his fists balled around two handfuls of his shirt.

"Dr. Delgado," he says, sounding alarmed. "I'm just doing my checks. I check every patient every hour."

"Bullshit. Try again."

My arm is heavy as I reach for the light on my bedside table. It takes me a couple seconds to switch it on, and when I do, I gasp with surprise.

It's Eric, a third-shift CNA.

"I saw you," Daniel grinds out. "I've got you on camera. That tape is going to the cops if you don't talk right fucking now."

"No." The panic in Eric's tone intensifies. "Please don't. I've got a new baby, and my girlfriend lost her job. I need this job."

"What was on that cloth you put over her mouth?" Daniel releases his hold on Eric but stays just a few inches away from him. Eric has to look up to meet Daniel's eyes because Daniel is so much taller.

Eric pauses before spitting out the answer. "Chloroform."

"Chloroform?" Daniel's tone is low and ominous. "Empty your pockets right now."

He holds out a hand, and Eric gives him an apprehensive look.

"I said *now*."

Eric reaches into the pockets of his scrubs and pulls out a tissue, his employee ID card, and a hypodermic needle.

"What is it?" Daniel asks.

"Sodium thiopental."

"You asshole."

Tears shine in Eric's eyes. "I'm sorry, Dr. Delgado."

"Who put you up to this?"

"I don't know his name."

Daniel gives him a warning look. "Tell me everything you do know."

Eric looks around nervously. "It was in May. Right after my

daughter was born. This guy came to my house and said he'd give me five grand to question Allison Cole. Another ten grand if I could get the answers he needs."

"And you decided to shoot her up with drugs to do it?" Daniel scowls at him.

"She's mute, man. What was I supposed to do?"

"You were supposed to report that visit to me, not take the money and abuse one of our patients."

Eric gives him a helpless look. "I didn't hurt her."

"Tell me more about the man who came to see you."

"He, uh . . . he's a black guy with perfect teeth. And a nose ring."

Eli. I know from Eric's description that it was Eli, who is Dax's right-hand man.

"How do you contact him?" Daniel asks.

"He gave me a phone number to call if I get the information."

"What information?"

Eric swallows nervously. "Who killed Allison's sister. And if she tells me that, where the book is."

"What book?"

"I don't know."

Daniel takes two handfuls of Eric's shirt and slams him against the wall.

"I don't fucking know, man," Eric says. "The guy told me I was on a need-to-know basis."

"Did you call him?"

Eric shakes his head frantically. "No. She never told me anything. All she does is say her own name over and over. Allison, Allison."

Daniel just stares at him for a second, and Eric pleads, "Please don't report me. I need this job so much."

"I don't need to report you. I'm in charge of all medical staff here. You're fired."

"No." Eric practically wails the word, tears welling in his eyes.

"Don't." Daniel's jaw ticks as he steps back and runs a hand through his hair. "You assaulted a patient. For money. You make me sick. You're damn lucky I'm not going to the cops."

"But . . . my girlfriend's car broke down, and—"

"Stop talking." Daniel takes out his cell phone and sends a text. "The night security guard will come get you and escort you off the property. And if you ever set foot on this campus again, I will take that tape to the cops."

Eric just sighs heavily and nods.

"How do you feel?" Daniel asks me.

I'm still groggy. I meet his eyes, hoping he'll get the message that I'm okay but still not fully myself.

"Drink some water," he says.

Within a couple minutes, a Hawthorne security guard comes into my room and responds to Daniel's instructions to escort Eric away. As soon as they're gone from the room, Daniel comes and sits down on my bed. He takes my hand, running the pad of his thumb over my knuckles.

"You okay?"

I nod, still in a haze.

"I have to go to Joanne Hawthorne about why I fired Eric. I'll ask her to keep it between us."

"What else are you going to tell her?"

He sighs softly. "I think I should tell her as much as you're comfortable with. You're in danger. We don't know what else this guy did, or will do, to try to get to you."

"It was Eli. He works for Dax."

Daniel's expression darkens. "You have to get out of here, Ava."

"And go where?"

His hold on my hand tightens. "Anywhere. I've got friends

who can hide you."

I shake my head, a new sense of determination taking over. "I want to go to Chicago."

"You can't do that. You won't be safe there."

"I need to go get the book and get it to the police. The only way I'll ever be safe from Dax is if he's in prison. That book has all the evidence they'll need."

Daniel can't disagree with me. His eyes are locked on mine as he thinks through what I said.

"I need to do this," I say, my throat tightening with emotion. "For Allison. Dax doesn't get to just live his life after what he did to her. So either I get that book to the cops . . . or I kill him."

"Or he kills you." Daniel arches his brows at me. "Have you even fired a gun before?"

I shrug. "I know it's not rational. But whatever I don't know . . . I'll figure it out. I'll learn. I have money."

"You can't do this on your own, Ava. I'm going with you."

I balk at his suggestion. "You have to be here. This place needs you."

"I've got plenty of vacation time. And Tillman can cover me."

My heart beats a little faster as I consider it. "But . . . what will you tell your boss?"

"Not the truth. Since Dax has gotten to at least one person who works here, I'll figure something else out."

"Are you sure you want to do this?"

"Yeah. But we're going to get the book and give it to the cops, not get into a shootout with Dax. And we do it my way."

"Okay." I squeeze his hand, hope warming me all over. "When?"

"Soon. Probably tomorrow." He looks at the clock. It's 3:45 a.m. "For now, get some sleep. I'll sleep in the recliner."

"I owe you. You've done so much for me."

He cups my cheek and leans close to me. "You've done a lot

for me, too. Maybe someday I'll be able to explain it all to you."
He kisses my forehead. "Now sleep, beauty."

I lie back, and he tucks the sheet around my shoulders. Even
when I close my eyes, adrenaline keeps coursing through my veins.

I still can't believe it. Dax sent Eli here. He knows I'm alive,
though he believes I'm Allison. He thinks I can identify the men
who killed my sister. He wants that book back.

Dax is a dangerous man. He's ruthless, and from what I saw
in that book, he takes out anyone who gets in his way. Or rather,
he has others do it. He doesn't like to get his hands dirty.

But I'm not scared of him anymore. My fear for my own life
died with my sister. I plan to look into Dax's eyes one more time
and see the same fear Allison did as the life bled out of her.

Allison died for me. If that's what it takes to get justice, I'll
willingly do the same for her.

Chapter
TWENTY-ONE

I HATE LYING to Joanne Hawthorne. She's been nothing but good to me since recruiting me to come here. And even though I've talked my way around telling her outright lies, I've lied by omission.

For starters, I didn't tell her Allison is really Ava. I trust Joanne, but I don't think there's any reason for her to know right now. Being hunted by Dax Caldwell is dangerous whether she's Allison or Ava.

But where I'm planning on taking her . . . that one got a little stickier. I told her I want to discharge Allison and take her to see a friend who I think can help her.

It's sort of true. I'll probably see Sam while we're in Chicago, and he probably can help her. Still, I'm not really coming clean, and she knows it.

"A friend who can help her?" Joanne asks me, her brow furrowed skeptically. "Is this friend a doctor?"

I sigh heavily. "The less I tell you, the better. Not just for me, but for you."

"I don't understand."

There's a knock on her office door, and someone opens it. It's

Heaton, who ignores me and looks at Joanne.

"You needed something from me?" she says.

"Yes, come in, Dr. Heaton."

Tension enters the room with her. Heaton sits down in the chair next to me, both of us looking at Joanne.

"Dr. Delgado thinks Allison Cole is ready for discharge," Joanne says.

Heaton's expression twists with disbelief. "What? She's still not even speaking."

"Silence doesn't mean she's mentally ill," I point out.

"Well, she went from being vocal and functional to completely silent."

"She experienced trauma."

Heaton looks back and forth between Joanne and me. "Yes, that triggered it. And she's not past it at all."

"How does a person ever get past that?" I ask.

I know from personal experience there are some things I'll never overcome. I live with the aftermath of my mistakes, hopefully, a better man now than I was then.

"Our philosophy is to get patients back to a functional, healthy place prior to discharge. Allison isn't there."

I shift in my seat, sensing that Joanne is going to side with Heaton. "What I want to do is try something new with her. I want to take her to see a friend of mine who I think can help her."

"Who? Where?" Heaton asks.

"Why does that matter?"

"Because I'm one of her treating clinicians. I should be told."

"I'll brief you when we get back. And then we can evaluate whether she's ready for permanent discharge."

Heaton shakes her head. "I'm not comfortable with this. I won't sign off on it."

"I don't recall asking you to."

Joanne interjects. "We want to have the entire medical team on board with decisions about patient care, Dr. Delgado. You know this."

I have to force myself to stay calm. "I'm the primary care physician here, and—"

"Which you remind us all of at every turn," Heaton cuts in.

I turn to her. "Frankly, your treatment of Allison has been wholly unsuccessful."

"Oh, and yours has been better?" Her tone is icy.

"Enough," Joanne says.

"We record Dr. Heaton's patient sessions, don't we?" I ask Joanne.

"Yes, why?"

"I think a review of her sessions with Allison will show that she's been unprofessional."

Heaton gets up from her chair. "That's outrageous. The unprofessional one is *you*. It's obvious you have feelings for Allison. And now you want to take her away from here for a trip with you, and you won't say where or why?"

I just look away. I've got no defense. I only want to protect the woman she thinks is Allison, but I can't be honest about why.

"That is *enough*," Joanne says firmly. She stands up behind her desk. "Dr. Delgado, I'm sorry, but I'm denying your request. I'd certainly be open to bringing a doctor or a therapist here if you think it would benefit Allison."

My shoulders drop with defeat as she turns to Heaton. "And Dr. Heaton, Dr. Delgado is in charge of the medical team here. Please treat him with an appropriate level of respect."

Heaton glowers in silence.

I can't help but make one last try with Joanne. "Allison is in danger here. You saw the tape."

"What tape?" Heaton asks.

"We have security," Joanne says. "I'll hire a personal security guard for her if I need to. But I can't square this in my mind, discharging her because of what happened with Eric."

"What?" Heaton looks back and forth between us. "What happened?"

Joanne answers. "Eric Hunt, one of our night shift CNAs, was terminated for assaulting Allison Cole last night."

"Assaulting her?" Heaton's eyes widen.

"Yeah," I mutter. "Acting unethically to coerce information from her. Can you imagine?"

The flicker of awareness in Heaton's eyes tells me I'm onto something. She swallows hard and shakes her head.

"I recommend upping security all around," I tell Joanne. "This place isn't safe for Allison."

"But now that Eric is gone—"

I cut her off, my tone frustrated. "How do we know he's the only one? The people looking for Allison could have gotten to others here, too. And next time we might not be lucky enough to catch them." I look at Heaton, hoping she feels the full force of my accusation.

"We can't overreact," Joanne says. "There was a threat, and you handled it. We'll increase security and address other threats as they arise. And I don't want this situation discussed outside this room. I'm not happy with staff sharing information with patients that shouldn't be shared. It can alarm them unduly."

"Then how will the staff know to be on the lookout for other suspicious activity?" I ask, looking at Heaton again.

"I think the increased security will also increase vigilance. If things change, we'll reconsider telling them. But for now, it stays here."

Joanne covers her mouth with her hand and looks out the window, her forehead wrinkled with worry. I know she was upset by the video I showed her of Eric putting chloroform on a cloth and pressing it over Ava's mouth. She said she'd hired him herself, and she felt like she'd failed at judging his character.

"Is there anything else?" she asks, sounding weary.

"No," I say.

"You're sure Allison is okay?"

"She's fine. I'll do labs on her today to make sure, but I'm not worried."

Joanne sighs softly. "I suppose I need to call her aunt and let her know."

"We should call the Chicago PD, too. I have a description of the man who bribed Eric."

Heaton looks downright ill. I'm more certain than ever that Eli paid her a visit, too. She makes a very nice salary here, though, so I can't fathom her needing the money.

"I'll take care of it," Joanne says. "And I'll call the security company."

"Tell them you only want people who have been employed there for at least a year," I say. "No new hires step foot in here. They could be in the pockets of the same people who bribed Eric."

"Right."

"What happened to Allison?" Heaton asks.

I stand up and head for the door. "I'll let Joanne tell you. I need to get back to work."

The adrenaline from last night still hasn't worn off. I've been in crisis-response mode this morning, making sure Ava is safe and trying to figure out how to get her out of here. I don't have the patience to deal with Heaton any longer.

I go to the staff lounge and pour myself a cup of coffee, taking the first sip as I walk out of the room and am stopped by a nurse named Carla.

"Dr. Delgado," she says, an apology in her tone. "Sorry, but I didn't know who else to come to about this."

If I had a buck for every time someone said that to me here . . .

My frustration is making me irritable, but I don't let it show. Most days, I'm glad the staffers know they can come to me about random stuff.

"Sure, what is it?" I ask.

"Leonard wants to update his will."

"Why?"

She shrugs. "He's been upset about people coming for him."

"Still the JFK thing?"

"I don't know. I can't follow him when he gets this upset. I feel really bad for him."

I nod and consider. "I probably need to adjust his meds. And in the meantime, do what he wants. Call Hawthorne's attorney in Greenville and ask her to come out today and see him about his will."

"Okay." She opens her mouth to say something, then closes it.

"What?"

"I just . . . don't you think we should remind him that he's safe here and there's no need to update his will?"

I take another fortifying sip of my coffee. "I do think we should reassure him that he's safe here. But he has every right to update his will."

"Even in a diminished mental state?"

"Yes. Most of his estate is locked down, but there are personal possessions and a little bit of money that he's allowed to change his mind on as much as he wants."

"A little bit of money?" Carla grins.

It's common knowledge here that Leonard is the sole heir to billions from his family's company. But his family attorney protected his estate a long time ago, so no Hawthorne employees can worm their way in with Leonard, thinking they'll get a cash windfall when he dies. It was smart that they not only did it, but also made sure the employees here knew it.

"It's probably more than a little bit to you or me," I say, shrugging. "And have one of the CNAs take Leonard horseback riding or let him work in his garden. Those things relax him."

"He's refusing to go outside because he says the hitmen are waiting for him out there."

"Damn." I sigh softly. "Okay. I have to do rounds, but I'll make some time after that to spend with him. Maybe I can get through to him. And I'll adjust his meds." I head toward my office, turning back to her on the way. "And you'll call the attorney?"

"Yes, Dr. Delgado."

I sit down in my office chair and finish my coffee, fatigue starting to creep in.

How will I break the news to Ava that she has to stay here? She's intent on getting justice for her sister, and she can't do it from the inside of a mental hospital. But my hands are tied. I tried and failed.

And how could I have left this place if Joanne had given me permission to take Ava? Issues like the one with Leonard just now pop up daily, and I don't know that I can just leave all of the decisions to Tillman. A week or two off is one thing, but who knows how long it would take us to get that book, get it to the cops, and see that Dax gets arrested? I know from my army days that the missions that sound the simplest often turn into much more.

As if my mountain of worries isn't tall enough, I remember Heaton's comments about me and the woman she believes is Allison. If she can see that I'm attracted to her, can others? Whether I act on it or not, it diminishes my credibility.

I get up from my desk, take my white coat from the hook, and put it on, then finish my coffee and toss the cup in the trash. My worries will have to wait, because I've got rounds to do.

Chapter
TWENTY-TWO

I JUST STARE at Daniel for a few seconds after he breaks the news. I guess I've come to see him as invincible, and it hadn't even occurred to me that there was someone here who could tell him no.

"Okay," I finally say.

"I'm sorry," he responds, shaking his head.

"Don't apologize," I whisper. "You saved my life last night. I know you did your best to get me out of here."

We're talking in a corner of the library, which is risky. But Daniel said we can't get caught alone in his office again because Dr. Heaton suspects his feelings for me. Guess the bitch is pretty perceptive.

It's only about twenty minutes before nine, which is lights out at Hawthorne.

Daniel keeps his eyes on the open doorway as he speaks. "We're bringing in extra security. I'll keep the camera running in your room, and I'll sleep in my office."

"But . . . for how long? I can't stay here, Daniel. Dax wants information from me, and he's not going to stop just because Eric couldn't get it."

"I know. But we need more time."

I shake my head. "I don't have time. He could get to the book and destroy it. Or the next CNA he pays off could inject me with something lethal to keep me quiet."

He exhales heavily. The fatigue on his face reminds me that unlike me, he hasn't slept in a while. As I napped in my room with Morgan on watch this morning, he was working and trying to get me out of here.

"Listen, let me worry about it," I whisper, wanting to touch him but afraid of risking it. "You've done enough."

He turns his face away from the door toward me, alarm swimming in his eyes. "You can't escape from here."

"I'm not asking you to help me or anything. I don't want to put you at risk."

"No, you can't."

Morgan walks into the library with Milo, smiling. She takes one look at Daniel and me and takes Milo's arm to leave.

"You *can't*," Daniel says again. "There's nothing but forest and mountains for hundreds of miles other than Greenville."

"Then I'll go to Greenville."

He shakes his head. "By the time you make it, there'll be photos of you up *everywhere*. You'll end up back here on lockdown in Level Three."

"There has to be a way."

Daniel crosses his arms, his expression tense. "There's not. This place was designed to prevent escape. There are motion detectors wired to alarms. You wouldn't even make it to Greenville, but you'd still end up on Level Three."

"Where are the motion detectors?"

His brows shoot up. "You think I'd tell you that? Listen to me, will you? There is *no* escaping this place. It's been here for more than fifty years, and people have tried. No one has succeeded."

I sigh, frustrated. "I have to at least try."

"Give me more time. Stay alert and let me figure this out. You need me to get to Chicago."

"But what if you can't get us out of here?"

"Oh, hey, Alexandra," Morgan calls out in a sing-song tone. Daniel and I step apart, both turning to the door just as a second-shift nurse named Alexandra walks into the library.

Thank you, Morgan.

"Dr. Delgado, you're still here," Alexandra says. "We need you on Level Three."

"I'll be right up."

She leaves the room, and Daniel turns back to me. "Don't do it. If you trust me, don't do it. Once you're on Level Three, you'll be at least sixty days from Level One. That's sixty days from any chance of discharge. Let me work on this."

I nod slightly.

"Say it," he prods. "Tell me what I need to hear."

Dammit. I can't deny him. "I won't try to escape."

"Thank you." He sighs with relief and reaches for me, but he pulls his hands away when they're just inches from my arms.

"Go," I say, sensing that he doesn't want to.

But he has to. Daniel is so integral to this place. Everyone looks to him for guidance. He's got a steady presence and a mind for problem solving.

That's why I know I have to listen to what he just told me, though it's hard. But he's right—I have to be smart about this. If I just jump, I may ruin my chances and endanger myself further. The thought of being locked down on the third floor—which Morgan calls Crazytown—is sobering enough to give me pause.

I sink down onto a leather sofa, gathering my thoughts, and Morgan walks into the room. Milo's not with her this time.

"So . . . how are you?" she asks, her brows lowered quizzically.

I look at her and offer a small smile.

"You know I've got your back, right?"

I nod, scooting over so she can sit down next to me.

"Because I feel like I saw your lips moving just now."

I just stare at her.

"It looked like you were talking to Daniel," she says. "Or maybe he was reading your lips or something?"

I shrug. She gives me a look that says she's not at all satisfied, but she moves on quickly in typical Morgan-fashion.

"Milo's bipolar." Sinking back against the couch, she puts her feet up on the dark wood coffee table. "He's got some rapid mood swings. It doesn't make me like him any less, though."

A CNA peeks around the doorframe and tells us it's fifteen minutes to lights out. One thing I definitely miss about my former life is not being sent to bed like a child every night.

"I need a favor," Morgan says in a low, conspiratorial tone. "Do you know where I can get some condoms?"

My mouth falls open with surprise.

"Not for right now," she says quickly. "Just . . . for later. Milo's still on Level Two, so it's not even an option yet. But when it is, I just want to be prepared."

I sigh softly. Of all the times to be silent. There are so many things I want to say to her about this.

"We can talk about it another time," she says, getting up from the couch.

I can't blame her for being lonely and quickly getting attached to the only male patient here who is close to her age and not on Level Three. But she's moving too fast.

The swell of protectiveness I feel for Morgan makes tears well in my eyes. I always felt this way about Allison, too. When Bryce Weaver pushed her down on the playground in first grade, ripping her dress and skinning her knee, I'd punched him in the gut so hard he cried.

I wasn't normally tough enough or strong enough to draw tears from the biggest kid in our class, but when I'd seen her crying and bleeding, that didn't matter. She made me tougher. She made me stronger.

And now I'm just me. Half of a whole. Growing up with an identical twin is like nothing else. Allison was my best friend. My shoulder to cry on and my constant cheerleader. She was my conscience. Neither of us was perfect, but between us, she was the good one. Always doing the right thing and putting others first.

It should have been me who died that night. Letting people believe I'm Allison has been easy because she's the one who deserves to live on. She didn't have a vengeful bone in her body.

I do, though. Dax should have just broken off our engagement. In sending men to kill me who accidentally murdered my sister, he woke a sleeping giant. And that giant is my love for my sister.

I won't let it pass. I'm stuck at Hawthorne Hill for now, bound by the promise I made to Daniel not to escape, but I won't be forever. I'm sane, and I've moved to a stage of grief that won't allow me to just feel despondent about Allison anymore.

Is there a stage of grief that includes plotting revenge by turning your ex in to the police so he can rot in prison? I'm on that one.

I SPEND THE next couple days working on Leonard's garden. What started as a patch of dirt is now worthy of that name. I've pulled the weeds that sprang up in his absence and enlarged the space a little, slowly tilling the earth by hand and sorting out the grass.

The garden is now five feet by three feet. I measured it as I expanded and am considering making it even bigger. Working outside is proving surprisingly therapeutic. The warm sunlight and cool earth make me feel alive in a way that's not painful. Out here, I don't feel alive at the expense of Allison. I just feel like a tiny square in a patchwork quilt of life.

My sister loved container gardening. She had a space on the roof of her apartment building where she grew peppers and strawberries. Tending to Leonard's space makes me feel a little closer to her.

He checks on me through a window from time to time, his expression lined with worry. Leonard is convinced there are assassins out here. I can tell when I talk to him that he's torn between not wanting them to get me and being pleased that I'm keeping up the garden.

I'm turning over the same patch of earth for the twentieth time, smoothing the soil and crushing the small lumps of dirt with my shovel, when I see Daniel approaching.

My pulse picks up at the sight of him. He's wearing gray dress pants and a dark blue polo shirt, his biceps testing the stretchability of the fabric. And of course, his trademark Timberland boots.

"How's it going?" he asks, one corner of his mouth quirking up in a smile.

I nod and smile back. It's best if I keep up my silence unless we're completely alone. I'm not ready to talk to anyone but him yet.

He twists open a bottle of water and passes it to me. I wipe the back of my hand across my sweaty brow and take it, drinking half of it. Guess I was thirsty.

"So I've got an idea with potential," he says in a low tone. "A former colleague of mine in LA is doing a four-week PTSD program. The next one starts in three weeks. I need you to write to your aunt and tell her you want to be in it. If I can get a request from her, I can convince the administrator here to let you go. You'll get weekends off, and I'll take a few days off while you're there and we can go to Chicago. We'll have to work fast, though. You'll have to finish the program and come back to Hawthorne after it's over."

I nod, feeling a glimmer of hope. I don't need much time. I know exactly where Dax's book is, and it's safe. All I need to do is get it and bring it to the police. I want to deliver it with my own hands and tell them everything I know about Dax and that night.

"Get me a letter for your aunt, and I'll send it out immediately," Daniel says.

I wipe my hands on my shorts and start gathering my gardening tools. I'm going to write that letter now. This has to work.

"Thank you," I say under my breath.

Daniel nods and takes some of my gardening tools, following me to the shed. When we're alone inside, I lay my palm on his forearm and meet his eyes, letting my feelings shine through. It's so good to let my guard down, just for a moment. His eyes are warm with affection, but there's still restraint in his expression. Even stolen moments here are risky.

"Someday, Ava," he says softly. "Someday, we'll be more than this."

Chapter
TWENTY-THREE

I ONLY MISS my bed a little. By the time I lie down on the couch in my office every night, I'm too exhausted to care where I'm sleeping.

It's been almost a week since Joanne turned down my request to take Allison, who is actually Ava, away. Ava wrote a letter to her aunt, and we're hoping for a quick response.

In the meantime, I've been on alert all the time. By day, I focus on work but am also looking for anyone or anything that seems suspicious. I sometimes go get a cup of coffee from the lounge just so I can find Ava and make sure she's okay. I wake up in the night and check my phone to make sure the camera in her room is working, fearing that the equipment failed and someone's in there hurting her.

That footage of Eric pressing a cloth over her face as she slept has stayed with me. Clearly, Dax has a high level of interest in that book, if he thinks the woman he believes to be Allison can lead him to it.

When the alarm on my phone rings to wake me up at 7:00 a.m., I realize I slept through the night for the first time in a while.

Must be why I feel decent.

I go to the Hawthorne gym and run a few miles on the indoor track, then lift weights. I can't help checking the camera feed in Ava's room on my phone a few times. She's still asleep, a light cover thrown aside, giving me a view of her bare legs.

Seeing her in the tank tops and shorts she sleeps in is a nice bonus to the camera in her room. I can so easily imagine her in my bed, her perfect round tits within reach if I slide my hand up her tank top. She doesn't wear a bra to bed, so does that mean she also doesn't wear panties? These are the questions I ponder when I let my mind wander from the important issue at hand, which is her safety.

After a quick shower in the gym's locker room, I put on my clean clothes, skip shaving, and head back to my office to get my coat and tablet for rounds. The Hawthorne housekeeping department has been doing the laundry they find in my office, which I'm not complaining about. Joanne offered to have them do my laundry all the time when I started here.

My rounds are pretty routine. Morgan asks me to prescribe the Pill for her to clear up her skin. Since her complexion is clear and she's been running around with the new bipolar patient, I'm pretty sure it's got nothing to do with her skin.

Leonard is quieter today, but I can tell from his expression there's still a war raging in his mind. His new antipsychotic meds take time to fully kick in, and in the meantime, he's left to remind himself that the things he believes to be true may not be. I hate seeing him suffer this way.

"Want to play some poker tonight?" I ask him over lunch.

He arches a brow and nods. Leonard loves poker. We play for small amounts of money, and he cleans me out every time. I think his mind tracks the cards and calculates the odds in a way I'll never be able to do.

"Bring your piggy bank, Doc."

"This is gonna be my night," I say, rubbing my hands together. "I can feel it."

He laughs, and it's the first time I've seen a smile reach his eyes in a while. "It's your night to lose, my man. I'd like to win that stethoscope of yours."

I look down at the stethoscope hanging around my neck. "What do you want with it?"

He shrugs. "I just think it'd look good on me."

I laugh and clap him on the back. "It would, but I've had this one since med school. I'm attached to it."

"Just your money will do, then."

We walk back into the great room. Light rain pelts the windows. It's been drizzly all day, so Level One patients who would normally be outside are all inside. I glance around the room for Ava and see that she's curled up on a couch with a book. She's not reading it, though, because Morgan is talking to her.

I go back to my office to catch up on paperwork. It never ends, but at least it gets more automated. I'm halfway through a state certification report when the sound of yelling makes me look up from my desk.

"They're coming! I knew they were!"

I recognize the voice immediately as Leonard's, and he's very upset. Without thinking, I grab my emergency sedation kit from my desk and run toward the great room. I never want to sedate a patient unless I have to, but if he's upsetting other patients, I may have to.

Leonard is yelling, telling everyone to run because the assassins are on their way. Patients are murmuring, and the nurse at Leonard's side is trying to console him.

"You're all right," I say to Leonard as I approach. "It's okay."

A loud bang sounds, and the double front doors fly open,

the wood frame splitting in places. Two men walk inside. They're dressed in black, wearing ski masks and carrying guns.

The patients' murmuring turns into gasps of terror. One woman bursts into tears.

"No one move," I say in a level tone.

The way the air stills in my lungs reminds me of some of the shit I faced when I was in the army. I assess things the same way I did then, looking for a way to neutralize these men without anyone getting hurt.

I'm reeling over Leonard's delusion coming to life and busting down the door when one of the men points his gun at the nurse next to Leonard, Cathy.

"Listen to the big guy. No one move." He flicks the wrist of his hand with the weapon toward the other man. "Up the stairs, then turn left. Fourth door on the right."

Ava's room. My blood runs cold. How the hell do they know exactly where her room is? The second gunman hurries upstairs. At least I know she's not up there.

"Hey, what's going on?" Tillman walks into the room and looks around.

"Don't move," the first gunman says sharply.

Tillman puts his hands up and keeps walking. "Are you guys robbing us? We don't have anything valuable here."

I use the time the gunman is focused on him to carefully reach into the sedation kit in my coat pocket and take out the needle.

"They're here for me," Leonard says with a scowl. "Took you assholes long enough to find me."

The gunman furrows his brow. "We're not here for you, old man. Shut up."

"I had nothing to do with JFK," Leonard continues. "You know that, though, don't you? This whole thing is one big setup."

"I said, shut the hell up, old man." The gunman gives him a

warning look.

"This is a mental hospital," I say. "Please just . . . remember that. No one here wants to piss you off."

"Room's empty," the second gunman calls from upstairs.

"Where's Allison Cole?" the first gunman demands, turning to me.

"She was discharged a few days ago."

"Bullshit." He turns the gun on me. "I know for a fact she's here. She was here this morning."

Patients are turning their heads toward Ava, and I cringe.

"There you are," the first gunman says.

He stalks toward Ava just as a security guard runs through the front door, his gun drawn. The second gunman, who is running down the stairs, shoots at him and misses.

Leonard moves fast, moving to stand in front of Ava.

"It's not her you want," he cries. "Leave her out of this."

I'm only about four big strides from the gunman. I've got two of them down when the gunman mutters, "I warned you, old man," and fires.

Ava screams as a bullet hits Leonard in the chest. I raise my arm and plunge the needle into the gunman's upper arm, tackling him to the floor at the same time.

When I look over at the other side of the room, the security guard is standing over the body of the second gunman, who is lying in a pool of his own blood.

The first gunman is struggling beneath me. I take his arm and pull it back at an odd angle, making him scream, though it's muffled because the sedative is working.

"Who told you where her room is?" I demand. "Tell me now, or I'll break your arm in a way that will never heal right. And then I'll break the other one."

"I can't . . ."

"Fucking tell me now," I grind out, pushing his arm almost to the breaking point.

He howls with pain, and I rip off his ski mask, revealing messy blond hair and tears streaming down his face.

"A . . . a lady doctor," he says in a high, panicked tone. "I don't know her name, I swear."

Heaton.

I push him to the floor, and he goes limp as I release his arm. Tillman is beside me.

"What should I do?" he asks. "We've called 911."

I take the gunman's weapon and pass it off to Cathy, the nurse. "Go give that to the guard. Tillman, send someone for restraints and tie this guy up till the cops get here."

He nods, climbing onto the gunman's back as I climb off. He's passed out from the sedative, but restraining him is a good precaution.

"You heard what he said about Heaton?" I ask Tillman.

"Yeah."

"Tell Joanne Hawthorne. And take care of this place while I'm gone."

"Gone?" He gapes up at me.

I walk over to Ava and move Leonard's body off of her. Once I have him on the floor, I check for a pulse, but there's nothing. He was hit in the chest and is bleeding heavily. Ava is sobbing, probably reliving her sister's murder right now.

Fuck. This whole scene traumatized every patient in here. We'll need to bring in counselors. It's not a good time to lose our psychiatrist, but I believe we just did. I'm not at all surprised Heaton was helping Dax, but I still don't understand why.

Two more guards walk into the room. The cops will be here soon. If I don't get Ava out of here now, I may not be able to.

"Come on," I say, taking her hand and helping her up.

Her pale pink shirt is soaked with Leonard's blood, and she's shaking. We don't have time for her to change or grab anything, though.

"We need to go," I say.

She nods numbly and follows me out the opening where the front doors used to be. I keep ahold of her hand as I run, leading the way to the garage where the Expedition is parked. I keep a spare key in my wallet, and I take it out and unlock the vehicle, helping Ava into the passenger seat.

I start it up and pull out of the garage, heading for the dirt road that leads to the highway. Ava's still sobbing next to me.

"Leonard," she says, her voice breaking with emotion.

I reach for her hand and squeeze it. "I know."

She turns to look at me. "Where will we go?"

I only hesitate a second before saying, "Chicago. After a stop by my friend Pike's shop in Greenville for a couple guns. I've got a bag of cash stashed under my seat for an emergency."

"Chicago," she says numbly.

"It'll be okay."

"As long as we get Dax, that's all that matters. I don't care if I die doing it."

My brows shoot up with alarm. "Well, I care a hell of a lot, so I'm not letting that happen."

She nods and wraps her other hand around mine as a new wave of tears strikes.

Leonard's dead. When I'm not in crisis mode, that'll hit hard. His illness haunted him to the end, but he still died a hero, protecting Ava.

For now, though, I can't think about any of that. I have to focus on getting Ava to safety, and then, on how we'll get that book and use it to bring Dax down.

Chapter
TWENTY-FOUR

NO MATTER HOW many miles Daniel puts between us and Hawthorne, I don't feel any distance.

Morgan is probably distraught. Same with June, the patient who burst into tears when the gunmen broke down the front doors this morning. I hope someone at Hawthorne is holding everything together and comforting people. Usually, that would be Daniel.

"What's on your mind?" he asks me.

"I go back and forth between thinking about Leonard and all the things I want to say to Dax."

Daniel's knuckles tighten on the steering wheel. "What kinds of things?"

"Oh, you know . . . I hate you, you should have been the one who died, you're disgusting . . . that sort of thing."

He pauses before asking, "Are there unresolved feelings?"

I turn to face him, shocked. "Are you asking if I still love him?"

"Not so much love as . . . I don't know. Just wondering."

"Daniel, I have no positive feelings for Dax, and I never will again. My only goal in life is to see him in prison until the day he dies."

He nods. Given what happened to Leonard, I know Daniel shares my goal.

We've been on the road for three hours now. Daniel stopped at a small gun shop in Greenville and bought a couple handguns, ammunition, and a clean T-shirt for me. It's a dark brown men's extra-large that's really big on me, has a giant deer head on it, and says "Nice Rack," but at least it's clean. The shirt I was wearing was soaked with Leonard's blood.

"We'll drive through the night and stop to sleep outside Chicago in the morning," Daniel says. "Joanne may have reported us to the police, so we have to stay off the radar."

"The police?"

He shrugs. "Technically, I'm probably abducting you right now."

"But how? I went willingly."

"Consent is different when you're in a mental hospital."

My stomach clenches with worry. "Wait . . . you're really going to be in trouble over this, aren't you? Will you lose your job?"

"I'll be okay."

"Daniel. We can turn around and go back right now if it will save you."

He shakes his head. "We can't do that. You're not safe there. And frankly, the other patients aren't safe with you there, either. We need to bring this to Dax's front step, not the other way around."

"But they need you there. I don't want you to get fired over this."

"One thing at a time, okay? Don't worry about that." He reaches over and takes my hand, and I study the dark ink on his forearm and wrist. "Can we get the book without tipping off Dax? Is it hidden near him?"

"No. He'd never find it where I left it."

"And where is that?"

I've never told anyone where the book is, and my heart pounds as I take a deep breath and say the words. "I asked my business partner Madeline to lock it in her safe."

"You think she still has it?"

"Yes. I trust her completely. We were friends for years before we started Brighton Cole. She didn't even blink when I asked her. She has my will and life insurance policies in her safe, too. I had hers in mine. We figured it was good to have each other keep them since we were co-owners in the business."

The rusty pickup truck Daniel borrowed from Pike lurches a little, and Daniel furrows his brow, shifting the gears until it's driving smoothly again. His Expedition is hidden in Pike's garage because Daniel didn't want to risk taking it. Now I know why—he's concerned the police could be after us.

"I think it's best if I go see her alone tomorrow to get it," Daniel says. "I'll have to tell her it's for Allison since she thinks . . . you know."

"She thinks I'm dead," I say softly.

He gives me an apologetic look. "You should lie low for now. We don't want to risk anyone seeing you or her telling anyone she saw you."

I sigh heavily and nod. I want to see Madeline, but I know he's right.

"When it's time for the police to arrest Dax, I want to be there," I say. "I have to see that."

"I understand. I'll make sure you're there."

We drive all day, only stopping to use the bathroom and get fast food. It's strange being with Daniel outside of Hawthorne, but in a good way. When we're in line at a gas station, he puts his arm around me and pulls me against him. I close my eyes, wrap my arms around his waist and hold on tight.

In Nebraska, we stop at a Target store about half an hour before closing time. We quickly cruise the aisles for essentials like toiletries. As we're piling clothes into a shopping cart, it hits me that I don't really exist anymore. I have absolutely nothing in this world right now—not even my own identity.

"I'll pay you back for all of this," I tell Daniel.

He shakes his head. "I don't want your money."

"I've got plenty, though."

"I do, too. Doctors aren't broke, you know."

I smile at his wry look. "I know. But I've got . . . I mean, I had . . . a fortune. I don't know how all that works now, though."

"Who did you leave everything to?"

"Allison," I say softly.

He takes my hand and squeezes it. "There's time to sort all that out later. I've got plenty of cash for everything we'll need."

I nod, but I don't like this feeling of dependence. My mother raised my sister and me to be independent in every way. I've come to rely on Daniel, but I don't like that he doesn't need me the way I need him.

I absently grab a nude bra in my size and toss it into the cart. I add in a pair of nude panties, blinking when I see Daniel putting a lacy black thong in the cart. He adds a white one, then picks up a sheer white camisole, nods with appreciation, and puts it in the cart, too.

"You like to cross-dress?" I tease.

He lowers his brows in a scowl. "Just making sure you've got plenty to choose from."

"Oh, yeah? Do I get to choose some underwear for you?"

"Sure." He smirks. "But I don't wear them to bed, just so you know."

"You don't wear . . . ?"

"Anything. I sleep in the raw, gorgeous. How about you?"

The moment of levity in our horrible day makes me laugh. "Guess that camisole will work."

He's reaching for a red camisole when an announcement about the store closing comes over the loudspeaker. Daniel pushes our cart to the checkout and pays for our stuff. As the cashier puts his underwear and mine in the same bag, I smile, because I like this.

As terrible as this day has been, Daniel came to the rescue. He's risking his job to keep me safe, help me find the book, and bring Dax down. The last time I had faith in a man, it ended in catastrophe. But I can feel Daniel's goodness down to my core.

Allison would love him. I wish she could have met him. And I wish he could have known her, too, because I was different when she was alive. I was tenacious and full of hope. Nothing felt impossible.

But since I lost her, I haven't cared what was possible. Even now, I can't imagine what I'll do when I get discharged from Hawthorne. Part of me doesn't want that. The people there only know what's left of me—the damaged, incomplete woman who sometimes hides within herself now. And they like me anyway.

When we leave Target, Daniel turns down my offer to drive. He's listening to talk radio news as we get farther from Hawthorne and closer to my hometown. At some point after midnight, I drift off to sleep.

I dream I'm covered in blood, and I'm trying to scream but no sound will come out of my mouth. When I jolt awake, Daniel puts his hand on my thigh.

"You okay?"

I slump back against the seat. "Yeah."

The clock on the dash says it's 4:05 a.m. I glance over at Daniel.

"I'm not tired," he says, reading my mind. "I've got my coffee and some BBC news on. This talk about international economies has me on the edge of my seat."

I smile, still looking at him. Everything about Daniel is big and muscular, from his neck to his broad shoulders and chest. He's kind of stuffed into this truck, which is smaller than the Expedition.

A sudden, deep yearning for him takes hold of me. I want him to pull the truck over so I can climb on to his lap. Being right next to him isn't close enough. I want to taste him and touch him and smell the coffee on his breath. As I look at his hand resting lightly on the steering wheel, I wish it were on me. His big, inked arms and hands turn me on like nothing else.

"What's on your mind?" he asks me.

He's on my mind, but I don't have words to explain how I'm feeling, so I say, "Nothing, really."

"Try to go back to sleep."

He pats my thigh again, and I swallow hard, wishing he'd move his hand higher. Slide it between my legs. This hard, sudden ache for him is overwhelming.

"I'm feeling . . . strange," I murmur.

Daniel furrows his brow with concern. "Are you feeling sick? We can stop if you need to."

"No." I blush just from my thoughts. "I've been attracted to you, since . . . well, you know, for a while."

He turns to look at me. "A while?"

"Yeah. I mean, it wasn't the moment I saw you, but soon after."

"And that has you feeling strange?"

"It's not that, exactly . . ."

"Ava, just tell me."

I take a deep breath. "I want you. Even though I know I can't have you. But God . . . I'm just craving you right now, Daniel. I want you on me and inside me. I want to feel you, and I want you to feel me. It's horrible because our friend was murdered today, but I want to have the hardest sex I've ever had in my life. With you. Right now."

"Fuck," he mumbles.

"I'm sorry. I know, it's—"

"It's really fucking hot. And I want you, too."

The air in the car thickens. My heart is racing, and I'm hot all over.

"Daniel," I say softly. "If we did, I wouldn't tell a soul. Not ever."

He licks his lips, and heat gathers between my legs. I want him more than I've ever wanted a man before. It's not just because of this moment, but all the moments that led us here.

"I don't want you to lie for me, Ava." He shifts in his seat and focuses on the traffic in front of us. "If we get involved on this trip, I'll accept the consequences."

"I don't want you losing your job over me."

He shrugs. "I don't want to lose you over the job, though."

I take his hand and hold it in both of my own. "You won't lose me just because we can't sleep together yet. Maybe it's just too soon. I'll get discharged at some point, and then—"

"Then you'll leave Hawthorne."

"I guess I'll have to."

"This trip, however long it ends up being . . . this may be the only time we get together like this," he says, a note of sadness in his tone. "And it's normal to want crazy good sex at a time like this. You're sad and angry, and you need a place to put those feelings. I feel the same way. And Ava, you're not having crazy good sex with anyone but me."

I smile, his words sending a warm tingle down my spine. "You're sure?"

"I'm so sure that we're stopping early." He glances over at an exit sign. "Here looks good."

"Leonard saved my life today," I say, my voice so soft it's nearly a whisper. "I'm alive. Do you know how many days out of the past few months I've spent feeling dead inside? I don't want to feel that way anymore. Allison wanted me to live . . ." I stop to take a breath, my throat tight with emotion. "And Leonard wanted me to live. I'm going to live."

Daniel brings my hand to his lips and kisses it. There's a neon sign for a rundown motel right off the interstate. He doesn't even ask me if it looks good because he knows I don't care. I'm exhausted in every way right now, but I need him.

I stay in the car while he goes inside to rent a room. He gets back in the car when he's done, and we pull around the back to park.

When we walk into the room, I'm pleasantly surprised. It's clean and has a nice king-size bed. It hits me all at once how grimy I feel. I wiped Leonard's blood from my arms in a gas station bathroom on the way here, but I need a shower badly.

Daniel takes the bag of toiletries into the bathroom, and I hear him turn on the shower. I click on the TV, deciding to find something to watch so I can stay awake and shower when he's done.

"You coming?" he asks, sticking his head out from the bathroom doorway. He's shirtless.

I'm halfway to the bathroom before his words even register. He had me at bare, muscled chest with dark hair and even more tattoos.

When I step into the small bathroom, it's filled with steam. It feels heavenly. Daniel takes hold of the bottom of my T-shirt and pulls it up and over my head.

"I really hate to see this go," he quips as he tosses my "Nice Rack" shirt to the floor.

He unfastens my pants next and pushes them down past my hips, bending down to reach. As they hit the floor, I reach for the fly of his khakis and unfasten them. His erection is every bit as huge as I expected, given his size. It springs out of his pants as I pull them down, taking his boxer briefs with them.

Daniel smells faintly of pine trees and coffee, with a hint of cedar mixed in. Steam swirls in the air around us as I breathe him in, my fingertips trailing down the lines of his chest to his hips. As soon as I get to his upper thighs, he inhales sharply and reaches for the back of my bra. It's stuck to my breasts, and he gently works the bloodstained fabric away from my skin.

I shimmy out of my panties and he drinks me in, his gaze that of a caged animal about to be set free. I used to get bikini waxes faithfully, but I'm not self-conscious about the dark curls between my thighs.

This is me. I'm alive. And Daniel and I need each other on a level that runs deeper than waxed bikini lines.

He opens the shower door, and a cloud of steam floats out. I take the hand he offers and step inside, the hot water feeling so good I moan with satisfaction.

Daniel steps in behind me and closes the door. He's got the soap and shampoo we bought, waiting on a ledge, caps open. I let the water run over my hair and down my face, washing away not just blood and sweat, but also my inhibition.

His hands wrap around mine and he turns me away from him, raises my hands in the air, and places them against the wall. My body tenses with anticipation as I wonder if he's going to take me right here and now. I hope so.

I can only see the white shower wall in front of me, but I hear him grab the bottle of liquid soap. He squirts some into his hands and lathers it, then puts his hands on my back.

An "ah" sound unconsciously rolls from my mouth at the feel of his hands on my bare skin. I shiver with pleasure as he slowly runs his hands up and down my back, to my neck, and then around to my front.

He washes my breasts, which seem small in his massive hands, and then rolls my nipples between his thumbs and forefingers as he lowers his face to the side of my neck and kisses it.

Tears of gratitude well in my eyes as he kisses me and massages my nipples. The hot water and his tenderness are the salve

I needed so badly. He takes his time, washing me everywhere. He even washes my hair, his erection brushing against my bare ass several times as he does it.

When I'm rinsed, I turn around, hoping to wash him. But he squirts some more soap into his palms and speed washes himself, finishing in thirty seconds and never taking his eyes off me.

When he turns off the shower and wraps me in a white bath towel, I feel more cared for than I ever have. Daniel knows what I need without words, because that's how he got to know me. He cared enough to learn my signals and read me.

His erection is sticking out in front of him like a foot-long steel pole. This whole time, he was putting me first, but now it's his turn.

I drop my towel to the floor and take his from him as soon as he's done drying his hair with it. Then I grab the box of condoms from the Target bag on the sink and lead him into the bedroom.

"I've wanted this for so long," I say, tearing open the box and handing him the roll of condoms.

"Me too." His expression is a mix of hunger and tenderness as he rips a package open and rolls a condom on.

I lie down on the bed and he follows, bending to kiss his way up one of my legs. I run my hands over his biceps, chest, and back, leaning up to meet him halfway. His mouth meets mine in a kiss that starts soft but soon turns deep and hard.

My body is wound tight with need for him, every part of me flushed with desire. I hope he can feel how much he means to me.

He enters me slowly, his eyes finding mine to make sure I'm good. I part my legs wider and moan as he fills me. His lips are parted, and he exhales deeply as he goes farther and farther inside me.

He's bigger than any man I've been with before, but he isn't hurting me. He goes slowly, letting my body adjust to him.

"Ava." He breathes out my name and buries his face in my neck as he thrusts into me.

"Yes," I whisper in his ear, wrapping my legs around his waist. "You always give me what I need, Daniel."

"Yes." His voice is full of emotion.

"Need me," I say softly. "Take me hard. Please. *Need* me, Daniel."

He groans and lifts his face to look at me, fucking me harder and faster now. "I do need you. I need you so much."

The physical pleasure mingles with the emotional gratification of his words, and I feel myself getting close to the edge.

"Oh, Ava." He grinds the words out, his expression twisted with pleasure and restraint.

I cry out his name, coming with the force of a hurricane. He's right behind me, groaning loudly and fucking me for another few seconds as we both ride out the last of our orgasms.

He moves off of me and tosses the condom to the ground, breathless. I immediately climb on top of him and pull the covers over us. Even now, I still need his closeness. I need to feel his warmth and tenderness.

"I'm gonna need more of that," I say, kissing his chest.

He laughs lightly and strokes my wet hair. "Yeah, me too. Give me fifteen minutes."

This sense of fullness and contentment can't last. But in this moment, I feel better than I have in a very long time.

Chapter
TWENTY-FIVE

I WAKE UP feeling relaxed and well-rested. The room is dark, and Ava is curled up against my side, her leg thrown over mine.

She's warm and soft and so damn tempting. I lift my head to look at the clock, wondering if I've got time to make love to her again before we leave.

It's 12:20 p.m. Guess not. I let my head drop down to the pillow.

We were up until almost nine this morning, exploring not just each other's bodies, but our first opportunity to be completely open with each other. Once I discovered her sleepy, sated post-orgasmic smile, I wanted to see it as many times as possible.

After Ava drifted off, I still had a hard time falling asleep because Leonard's murder was running through my head on repeat. He was such a good man, and he didn't have to die. I'm really fucking angry over it. I watched too many people die needlessly in war. Hawthorne is a place of healing, and those hired guns eroded the safety patients feel within its walls.

That's why I gently ease myself away from Ava, setting aside my desire for her. I have to get Dax's book so we can meet up with my friend Sam tonight and turn it over.

She sits up and looks at me, her dark hair a beautiful mess. My cock stiffens at the sight of her round, perfect breasts. I love how confident she is, not covering herself with a sheet, just letting me look my fill.

As if I could ever be full of her.

"See something you like?" she asks softly.

I smile and grab a T-shirt from the bag of clothes on the dresser, ripping the tag off. "If I get back in that bed, I won't get out until tomorrow."

She groans and steps out of the bed. "I know. And as heavenly as that sounds, I guess we need to get on the road."

I can't take my eyes off her as she stretches her arms upward and walks to the bathroom. Everything about her is smooth, soft, and sexy. I'd really love to feel her sweet little body on top of me again before we leave. She rode me like a fucking porn star earlier, digging her nails into my skin as she came.

But I can't think about that now. I've got to keep my mind on getting the book. Well, first some coffee, then the book.

I put on my jeans, brush my teeth, and tame my morning hair. Ava dresses, brushes her teeth, and pulls her hair back into a ponytail. There's a catch in my throat as she smiles at me from across the room. She's just packing our clothes into a plastic Target bag, but the look on her face is one I'll never forget. She looks content and hopeful. She's girl-next-door gorgeous, and her smile is for *me*. It was *me* who fucked her into contentedness and gave her hope of justice for Allison's and Leonard's murders. And I won't let her down. Whatever it takes, I won't see her disappointed. Not now. Not ever.

We hit a drive-thru for sandwiches, and I get the coffee I'm craving. I'm feeling pensive as I get back on the road to Chicago.

The care I feel for Ava stirs up memories of my relationship with my ex-wife. My love for Julie developed over time. We drifted into love as we got to know each other. This thing with Ava feels more like falling hard and fast, with no regard for how unlikely it is we can be together long-term.

I can't see a scenario in which we work out. If I get fired, which is probable, I'll have to get a job somewhere else. If she gets discharged, which is also probable given the progress she's made, she'll have to move somewhere else.

But how do I go back now?

"I was a bad husband," I say out of nowhere, both to Ava and to myself.

"How so?"

I sigh softly. "I put work first. Residency is demanding, but I worked harder than I had to. I wasn't there for Julie."

"Did she tell you she needed more from you?"

"Yeah. And the more she complained about it, the further I withdrew. I felt like I was in a pressure cooker. There weren't enough hours in the day to be the doctor, husband, and father I wanted to be."

"Is that when she left you?"

I shake my head. "No. First, she started having an affair with one of our coworkers. A cardiac surgeon."

Ava makes a soft sound of sympathy. "I'm sorry."

"Don't be." I glance at her, then quickly back at the road. "Julie was lonely, and I was too wrapped up in my work to care. I'm not saying I deserved it, but . . ." I shrug. "I guess I did deserve it."

"No one deserves that."

I shift in my seat, the memories making me uncomfortable. "After she left with Caleb, that's when I started drinking. I'd have a drink occasionally before that, but I started drinking heavily. I wasn't able to cope with my feelings of failure."

"How did that affect your work?"

Regret swells inside me, so powerful I have to force it back. "It wasn't good."

She reaches over and puts a hand on my thigh, silently reassuring me.

"People put me on a pedestal at Hawthorne," I say. "But I don't deserve it."

"Sure you do."

I shake my head. "I've made mistakes, Ava. Big mistakes. The guy you met back in Montana, the infallible doctor, he doesn't really exist."

"I don't think you're infallible."

"But you see me as . . . capable."

"More than capable." The warmth in her voice reaffirms my concerns.

"I like the way you look at me," I admit. "Like I hung the moon."

"To me, you did. And I like the way you look at me. Like I'm all right just the way I am."

I balk at that. "You're so much more than 'all right.' You're perfect."

"I'm not, though," she says softly.

"Perfect in my eyes."

I take her hand and bring it to my lips, kissing it. I need to tell her the whole truth about me. She deserves to have the last piece to my puzzle. But I'm selfishly going to hang on to her adoration for me a little longer.

We make it to the Chicago suburbs a little after three in the afternoon, and I take Ava to a hotel, where we'll stay tonight. I walk her to the room, and she gives me a piece of paper with the address of the Brighton Cole offices on it.

"Don't be long, Dr. Lumberjack," she says as I turn toward the door.

"I won't." I smile and take one last look at her. "Lock up behind me."

I wait outside the door to make sure I hear her locking the deadbolt. Then I set out for the city, where the traffic reminds me of life in LA. I already miss the wide-open sky and quiet of the Hawthorne property. I hope Tillman's holding down the fort.

Brighton Cole's offices are downtown in a skyscraper. The entire second floor belongs to the company, and I'm immediately impressed when I step off the elevator.

It's a large, open office with floor-to-ceiling windows. Desks and partially dressed mannequins are scattered around the room. The walls are painted a bright shade of orange.

"Can I help you?" a woman at a reception desk asks.

She's young and well-dressed, wearing a dark green blouse with her hair pulled up. I don't miss her inspection of the ink on my arms.

"I'm here to see Madeline Brighton."

Her smile tells me I must be new here. "I'm sorry, Miss Brighton is—"

"It's about Allison Cole. I don't need long."

The receptionist's eyes fill with sadness. She glances over at a wall of offices and then down at the phone on her desk. "Let me see if she's off her call."

She picks up the phone and relays the message to Madeline, who apparently tells her to send me right in.

"Last door," the receptionist says, pointing.

I hear chatter about hemlines, boots, and purchase orders on my way back to Madeline's office. This seems like a laid-back, creative environment, but it's hard for me to picture Ava here.

Madeline is waiting at the door when I get to her office. She steps aside and I walk in.

She's got shoulder-length blond hair, and she's wearing a black pencil skirt with a matching jacket. I try to picture Ava in the outfit, but I just can't.

"Madeline Brighton," she says, closing the door and offering me her hand.

"Hi, I'm Daniel Delgado." I shake her hand, and she gestures at a leather chair in front of her desk. I sit down.

"I'm a friend of Allison's," I say.

"How is she? Is she still in New York with Maggie?"

I shake my head, wishing I had thought about my answers to questions like this before I got here. "She's doing well. She left New York and is just doing some R and R right now."

"Good. I've been worried about her. We all have. What happened to Ava was just . . ." She looks out the wall of windows and clears her throat. "It was awful. I miss her."

"I'm sure."

She turns to look at me. "Did you ever meet Ava?"

I've got no choice but to lie. "No, I didn't."

Madeline smiles. "She was like . . . a light. A bright light that never goes out. Always thinking, always innovating. You don't really think a light like that can ever be dimmed, and then when it's just *gone* . . ." She sniffs and takes a deep breath. "I'm sorry. You didn't come here to hear me talk. Is there something I can do for Allison?"

"Yeah, actually. She said Ava told her that you're keeping some stuff in your safe for her. Allison would like those things."

Madeline's brow furrows with concern. "I sent the will and life insurance stuff to Ava's attorney a few weeks after she died. I didn't know what else to do with them."

"Okay. What about the book?"

Madeline leans her elbows on her desk. "The book?"

She knows what I'm talking about. I can see it on her face.

"Yes. The one Ava gave you the day before she was murdered. It's black."

She nods. "Right. Well, like I said, I tried to send Ava's stuff to the right place after she died. I didn't see any reason for me to keep it."

"So Ava's attorney has the book, too?"

"No." Madeline meets my eyes, and I swear I see a flicker of challenge. "I gave the book back to Dax since it was his."

Chapter
TWENTY-SIX

THE SLIDE AND beep of Daniel running his key card through the reader on the hotel room door makes my pulse speed up, even though I knew he was coming. He texted me that he was in the parking lot and on his way up a couple minutes ago, so I unlocked the deadbolt. He was only gone a couple hours, but I missed him.

I get up from the chair I was sitting in and meet him halfway across the room. His lips are set in a thin line of disappointment.

"What happened?" I ask, deflating.

"She doesn't have it."

I just stare at him for a second, dumbfounded, and then a wave of dizziness hits. "Doesn't have it? How can she not have it? I gave it to her. I watched her put it in her safe."

Daniel puts an arm around my waist and walks me to the edge of the bed, where we both sit down.

"I'm sorry," he says, taking my hand.

I shake my head, still not understanding what's happening. "Where's the book? I need that book, or I have nothing on Dax." My voice is high and frantic.

"There's no easy way to say this. She gave the book to Dax."

"What?" I shrink back, bile rising up my throat.

"She said she sent your stuff where she thought it should go after . . . your death. Your attorney has the will and insurance stuff, and Dax has the book."

"But I never told her it was his. I didn't tell her a single thing about that fucking book. I just told her it was important."

I bury my face in my hands and let the tears take over. This is what I get for having hope. Being punched in the stomach would hurt less than this.

Daniel puts his arm around my back and pulls me against him. I cry like I never have before. My shoulders shake with sobs and snot drips from my nose, but who fucking cares?

I've never felt so hopeless. Allison was viciously murdered before my eyes. She knew she was dying. She died suffering and struggling to breathe on my kitchen floor. She died in my place.

And the only leverage I have on Dax is gone. How could Madeline give it back to him? The thought sends a sick chill down my spine. She read it. Just that was a violation. But to return it to him when I was murdered a day after I asked her to keep it safe?

That's more than a violation. My sadness morphs into anger that quickly becomes full-on rage.

"Where are the guns?" I ask Daniel, sitting up and meeting his eyes.

"Why?"

"Where are they, Daniel?" My voice is nasally from crying. I reach for a tissue on the nightstand and wipe my nose.

"The guns are safe. And since I'm the only one of us who knows how to use them, why do you need to know where they're at?"

"That book was my only shot at getting Dax sent to prison. And the thing about realizing I want to be alive is that I know I can't live a life where there's no justice for what he did to Allison."

"So you want to kill Dax."

I nod. "More than I've ever wanted anything. I also want the guy who . . . who . . ." I'm crying again, and I can't speak past the lump in my throat. I take a deep breath and continue. "The one who killed her. He deserves to die, too."

"He does. So does Dax." Daniel squeezes my hand. "But that would go bad, Ava. You'd end up dead before you could even get your finger on the trigger. I can't let that happen."

"It's not up to you."

"I know this isn't what we were expecting, but let's just let it settle and talk over our options."

I stand up, clenching my fists at my sides. "There are no options! There's only one thing left. And if Dax kills me before I can kill him, at least he'll go to prison for that. I'm not afraid of dying. If I die avenging my sister, I'll die in peace."

Daniel stands up and pulls me into his arms. I push on his chest, resisting the comfort. I don't want comfort now. I only want the fury that will fuel me to act and finally end this. Dax has been living these past few months, drinking and eating and fucking his way through life while Allison rots in the ground and I live through hell. No more.

"Come on," Daniel says softly. "Hey. It's okay."

I have no hope of pushing free of his embrace. It feels good to fight it, though. To have something to shove and curse and be angry at. My hands only meet hard muscle that doesn't even flinch under my punching and scratching.

"Why would she do that to me?" I bury my face against his chest and scream into his shirt. "Who can I even trust anymore?"

"Me." Daniel holds me tight, and I go limp against him. "You can trust me, Ava."

"Let me do this," I say softly. "Give me some money and a

gun, and get in the truck and drive back to Hawthorne. I don't want you around when I do this."

"You're not doing it." He smooths my hair and kisses my temple. "And I'm not going anywhere. We're meeting Sam at seven tonight."

I lean back and look up at him. "Why? We don't have the book to give him."

"Just to consider options." He cups my face in his huge hands. "Trust me, okay? We've got the advantage here. We just need to be smart."

"How do we have the advantage when he has the book?"

Daniel leans his forehead against mine. "We're the only ones who know you're still alive. We're going to talk over our options, make some plans, and even wait if we have to. I'll break in to his house and steal the fucking book if I have to."

"You really think we can still do this?"

"We'll figure something out. I promise."

I nod. "Okay."

He leans his head back until our eyes are locked. "Promise me you won't do anything stupid."

"I won't."

"I've never broken my word to you, and I never will."

"I know." I smile as he brushes the tears from under my eyes. "And I'll never break my word to you, either."

He turns to look at the clock. "We need to leave for dinner in half an hour." After leaning in to kiss me, he smiles. "How can we get you relaxed by then?"

My stomach flips with excitement. "Show me what you've got, Dr. Lumberjack."

His laugh is low and sexy. "You know what I've got, Miss Cole. But I haven't even begun to show you what I can do with it."

DANIEL RELAXED ME very well—*twice*, and I'm feeling a little less homicidal when we walk into an Italian restaurant near our hotel.

A muscular man with close-cropped blond hair approaches Daniel with a grin. They give each other a man hug, complete with back slaps and wry insults.

"You forget the rest of your hair back at the office, suit?" Daniel jabs at Sam.

"Fuck off, man. I see some silver in your temples."

Sam's wearing a dress shirt and tie, his biceps testing his shirt's limits. He turns to me with a warm smile.

"It's great to meet you, Allison," he says softly. "I'm sorry about your sister."

"Thank you. It's nice to meet you, too."

He shakes my hand, and I immediately like him. We're led to a table in the back, and I just enjoy listening to the two men catch up for a few minutes. I've only seen Daniel in doctor-patient interactions at Hawthorne, and I like this relaxed, unguarded side of him. His smile is easy and he laughs. When he puts his arm around my shoulders, I feel like some of his warm demeanor seeps into me, wearing away at my urge to take out Dax immediately no matter the cost.

I still want him dead or locked up. But Daniel's right—we need to be smart about it.

After the small talk is done and we've all ordered, Daniel rubs my shoulder reassuringly and clears his throat. I think it's time to do what we discussed on the way here.

"Uh, Sam," he says. "There's something you need to know, but it has to stay between the three of us."

Sam lowers his brows and nods. "If it involves laws being broken, don't tell me."

"It doesn't." Daniel turns to me. "I trust this guy with my life. You can tell him."

My heart hammers nervously as I get up from my chair, walk over to Sam's side of the table, and sit down beside him. I lean in close and relay the truth of my identity in a hushed tone. His breath catches when I tell him who I really am.

"No fucking way," he says in a low tone.

When I'm finished and I lean back over to the seat, he meets my gaze, sympathy etched on his face.

"I'm so sorry," he says.

Daniel jumps in, speaking in the same near-whisper Sam and I are. "Don't call her by name or say anything that could—"

"I got it," Sam says, nodding. "I understand."

I move back over to sit by Daniel, sliding my hand into his. He squeezes it and speaks to Sam.

"So I went to get the book today, and Madeline told me she gave it back to Dax."

Sam winces. It's subtle, but I see it. After a heavy sigh, he says, "It might not have held up anyway. Caldwell's an elusive son of a bitch. He always manages to skate."

"There has to be another way," I say, a pleading note in my tone. "I know who some of the people he deals with are. Maybe you could threaten them with arrest to get them to testify against him?"

Sam's expression is grim. "We haven't found anyone willing to roll over on him yet. It's not that we don't know what he does, it's that we can't prove it in court."

"What about stealing the book back?" I suggest. "I know where he usually keeps it."

"I'm guessing it's always close to him, though," Sam says.

I nod. "But I'll do whatever I have to do to get it. I'm not afraid. I'll break in if I have to."

Sam starts to shake his head, and Daniel says, "No fucking way. We already talked about this."

"We're talking about options," I say. "And that's an option.

What else do we have?"

Sam leans forward, his elbows on the table. "Do you want to keep your identity a secret?"

I look at Daniel. "I don't care about that anymore. When he finds out who I am, Dax will want me dead. But as long as I can bring him down with me, that doesn't matter."

"The hell it doesn't," Daniel says, his tone aggravated. "Will you stop trying to—"

Sam interrupts him. "Guys, I'm not suggesting that she go in there on her own. But what if . . ." He looks from side to side, making sure no one is in earshot, then meets my eyes across the table. "Would you be willing to wear a wire? If you can get him on tape admitting he hired those two guns, then we'll have something solid."

"Yes." I say it without hesitation.

Daniel shifts in his seat. "I don't like this. It's too dangerous."

"I'd be outside in a surveillance van with a SWAT team," Sam says.

"It would take *one second* for him to kill her," Daniel fires back. "And who gives a shit if your SWAT team busts down the door and she's dead?"

"You want me to send someone in with her as protection?" Sam offers.

"Yeah. Me."

Sam gives him a skeptical look. "You're a doctor. When's the last time you fired a gun?"

"Last weekend when I was hunting."

"Yeah, but—"

"It's me or we're not doing it," Daniel says firmly. "I'll do whatever it takes to keep her safe."

"Our guys are trained to put her first."

Daniel leans forward. "It's me or no one."

I touch his arm, and he turns to face me.

"Why risk both of us instead of just one?"

He narrows his eyes, and I see a flicker of hurt cross his face. "We go in there together or not at all. If you want me on board with this crazy-ass plan, that's my condition."

"But—"

"I love you. And I'm not losing you."

The raw emotion in his voice brings tears to my eyes. "Oh, Daniel. I love you, too. And there's no one I trust like you."

He nods and turns back to Sam, who is trying to look like he wasn't listening to us just now.

"So get it set up, then. We're in."

Sam sighs, his forehead creased with reluctance. "Okay. Probably tomorrow night, at his home."

"Thanks, man," Daniel says.

"I have to get it cleared with my boss."

"You will."

Sam scoffs and smiles. "Yeah, I should be able to."

Our food arrives, and my stomach growls painfully at the scents of fresh baked bread and cheesy pasta. I'm so hungry.

"One more thing," Daniel says as we all start eating. "Can you find out if there's a missing person report or an abduction report for her?"

Sam sets his fork down. "Hey, motherfucker, you didn't mention you're a fugitive."

"I might be." Daniel puts a forkful of lasagna in his mouth. "That's what I need you to find out for me."

"I'm gonna be bailing your ass out of jail again, aren't I?"

Silence falls over the table.

Again? Sam has bailed Daniel out of jail before? From their expressions, I can tell it wasn't a small thing.

"Sorry," Sam murmurs.

"It's okay." Daniel turns to me. "I'll tell you about it later."

Sam shakes his head and looks down. "I'm an asshole. I shouldn't have said that."

"It's fine," Daniel says shortly. "Just check and see if I'm wanted, will you?" He reaches over to Sam's plate. "And give me your garlic bread. It's the least you can do."

The rest of our dinner passes in uncomfortable silence or tense, short conversation. I'm relieved when we part ways in the parking lot, Sam promising to text Daniel as soon as he knows something.

I'm feeling shaken up on the drive back to our hotel. Daniel is good and honest. I can't imagine him doing something that would land him in jail. And from his drawn expression and his death grip on the steering wheel, it's something he's ashamed of.

The man I'm in love with may be tumbling off that pedestal soon. I'm once again questioning my judgment with men, hoping I haven't fallen in love with another criminal.

Chapter
TWENTY-SEVEN

WHEN I WAS in the army, I once did one-handed chest compressions on a wounded soldier while firing at insurgents with a gun in my other hand. I didn't miss, and my patient lived. I'm not saying I'm perfect by any means, but I've got my strengths. I'm a good guy for anyone to have in their corner. I pride myself on being strong and solid.

But it only takes a single bottle of booze to bring me to my knees. I'm sitting on the edge of the bed in the hotel room, elbows on my knees, my temples sweating, and my pulse pounding.

I could smell the alcohol when we walked past the bar in the hotel's lobby, and it was like a reunion with a long-lost friend. All my memories of things I did after drinking are bad, but the memory of the way that first drink always went down is the most powerful.

The first drink made my problems seem smaller. The second made me feel like maybe life wasn't so bad after all. And by the third, I was always feeling good. I never felt any incentive to stop after three, though.

Ava is taking a bath right now, and without her here beside

me, my attention has shifted to the bar. I could run down there really quick and have a shot. It would calm me. Smooth things out. Maybe make it easier to have the dreaded conversation with Ava about why I was arrested.

Fuck. I can't drink. I can't go back there. I've got no self-control once I start.

I run my hands through my hair and sigh heavily. This is what I'll be up against every day if I get fired from Hawthorne. I'll end up at an urban hospital with bars near home and work.

A deep stab of contempt runs through me, slicing hot and fast. I'm supposed to be strong and steady for Ava, but here I am sweating and practically shaking over my urge to drink.

"Hey," she says, smiling as she steps out of the bathroom.

There's a white towel wrapped around her body and another around her hair. As she approaches me, all thoughts about the bar downstairs disappear.

Her fresh coconut smell fills my consciousness as she stops between my knees, and I sit up straight on the edge of the bed. Her hands go to my shoulders, mine go to her waist.

"You love me," she says softly, her brown eyes warm as she looks down at me.

"Yes." I tighten my hold on her hips.

"So show me."

My body reacts in an instant, my cock hardening as I grab the towel to pull it away. But she stops me by covering my hands with hers.

"Tell me why you were arrested, Daniel. Loving me means trusting me."

A heavy sigh escapes my chest. "You're right."

She cups my bristled jawline, her thumb brushing over my lower lip. "I don't mean trusting me with the information," she says, her voice like warm silk. "Trusting that I'll still love you.

Because I will."

"You see me as a man who puts others first." I grip her waist again and lean forward, resting my forehead against the towel below her breasts.

"Because you do."

"But there was a time when I didn't."

She runs a hand through my hair and down to my neck. "You already told me you fell short of the husband and father you wanted to be. I've fallen short, too. Allison might still be alive if I had trusted her instincts and not been so selfish."

I lean back and look up at her. "It's not that simple, Ava."

"It's probably not that simple with you, either."

She looks down at me, her gaze filled with expectation and adoration. I soak it in, wondering if I'll ever see it again. And then, I begin.

"I told you I was drinking heavily after Julie took Caleb and left me. I'm not going to make excuses about why I drank, because no matter how stressed and hurt I was, I should have acknowledged there was a problem and gotten help. I'm a doctor, and the drinking was starting to impair me. I'd go into work hungover, and halfway through my shift, I'd be counting the hours until I could get drunk again." I shake my head, loathing the man I was then. "So one night . . . I treated a patient who came into the ER complaining of abdominal pain. I ran the usual tests, but I couldn't find anything conclusive. It was close to the end of my twenty-four hour shift, and I was starting to feel shaky and . . ." I blow out a disgusted sigh. "I was a drunk. My body needed its fix. And I discharged the patient without completing the final few tests I should have run to rule out internal bleeding. I didn't want to work over and wait for the results. After work that night, I was pulled over and arrested for drunk driving. My patient . . . died at home that night." I close my eyes, fighting past the lump in my throat. "It all came to a head when I was arrested. My medical license was suspended, and I ended up in rehab to avoid jail time for the DUI."

My shoulders sink with relief. No matter what happens from here, she knows the worst of me now. I thought I didn't want that, but the pressure inside me has released.

"I'm sorry you went through that," she says, cupping my face in her soft hands.

"Don't be sorry for me. Be sorry for the man who died because of me."

She nods. "I am. But you're human, Daniel."

"Don't defend me." I clear away the gravel from my throat. "I took an oath to do no harm, and I killed a man."

"You didn't kill him."

"I didn't catch the thing that killed him, and that was my job. He eventually would have died from the bleeding anyway, but I could have given him a chance to say goodbye to his family. Maybe just a little more time. Something."

She leans forward and kisses my forehead. "Having life and death in your hands every day is a very heavy burden."

"I was impaired, and I knew it."

"You paid a price, though."

I scoff. "Not enough of one."

"And that's how you ended up coming to Hawthorne?"

"Yeah. Joanne Hawthorne recruited me when I got my license back. She told me they have trouble finding quality doctors willing to relocate to the middle of nowhere, no matter how much they pay. But for me, it worked. I didn't want to go back to a busy ER environment. I wanted a chance to reinvent myself, and I thought I could make a difference at Hawthorne. Mental illness is unfairly stigmatized. And as a veteran and a recovering alcoholic, I know what it's like to battle demons."

"You do make a difference there. You know that, don't you?"

I shrug. "I try to. But it'll never be enough to atone for my wrongs."

"How can you know? Maybe you're saving more lives at Hawthorne than you realize. It's a hard thing to quantify."

She's not disgusted with me. I was expecting at least a little judgment, but there's none. It reminds me again how lucky I am to have her in my life. I slide my hands from her waist around to her ass, cupping it through the damp towel.

"I never expected more than what I had." I look up at her. "I'm starting to rebuild a relationship with Caleb; I had my work and my weekend hiking trips. I thought it was enough. But then you came along."

It only takes a single pull on the front of her towel to make it drop to her feet. My eyes drag down her body slowly, from her round breasts and pink, pebbled nipples, down to her smooth stomach and then between her thighs.

"You looking at me makes me hotter than other men did touching me," she says softly.

I hate that other men have touched her. There's no way any of them has felt the same reverence for her that I do. And now that I've had her, I can't go back.

"I swear you were made for me, Ava." I tip my head back to look up into her eyes, fighting the urge to jump up from the bed and fuck her up against the wall. "Just for me."

I swipe my tongue gently over one of her hardened nipples, then swirl the tip of my tongue around it, making her shiver. When I slide my hands back to her ass and cup it, her skin still warm from the shower, she inhales sharply. I squeeze harder and she moans.

"You were made for me, too, Daniel," she says, her voice breathy and soft. "You knew me before I'd even spoken to you."

She pulls on the back of my T-shirt, and I raise my arms to help her get it off. Then she puts a knee on the bed, and we fall back together, her straddling me.

When she kisses me, her hair brushes my shoulder. She tugs my lower lip between her teeth and I groan, gripping her hips and pulling her down against me.

"Did you think I'd stop loving you?" she murmurs. "I *can't* stop, Daniel. You're a part of me now."

Warmth radiates through my chest. The only need consuming me now is for her. She unfastens my jeans and slides them off, the bouncing of her tits making my balls ache with lust.

I'm working my legs out of my pants as she grabs a condom from the nightstand and tears it open, her expression intent as she slides it down my erection. I groan from the feel of her fingers on me.

I never thought I'd have this. Living at an isolated mental hospital, where I'm only around patients and staff, I never thought I'd have any sort of partner again. I didn't even consider a fuck buddy an option. But someone who sets me aflame with her touch? A woman I'd walk through fire for? I didn't even hope for someone like Ava.

She straddles me and makes fast work of situating my tip at her opening, then sinking down onto me. We groan in unison.

It's hotter than any fantasy I could imagine. Ava rides me hard and deep, using my cock for her satisfaction. Her mouth is halfway open in a perpetual state of bliss. Every time she says, "Oh, God" or "Daniel," I have to force myself to hold back. It takes self-control not to grab her hips and pound myself into her. She's tight and wet, and watching her take pleasure from me is the hottest thing I've ever seen.

We're both survivors, she and I. I survived my own mistakes and their fallout, and she survived a deep, violent loss. But pain doesn't care about fault. It seeps into our bones and becomes a part of us whether we want it to or not. Whether we deserve it or not.

Whether we feel strong enough to handle it or not.

She's grinding against me, moaning as she gets close to climax. It's a beautiful thing, two survivors finding release and hope in each other. When she comes, I grind my teeth, holding on to my own orgasm until she's coming down from hers.

With a sated smile, she falls on top of me, breathless. I stroke her wet hair for a few seconds, as content as I've ever been.

"I was going to tell you anyway," I say.

"Hmm?" She turns to face me.

"About the DUI and the license suspension. I didn't only tell you because Sam let it slip at dinner."

She leans up on an elbow and kisses me softly. "I know you would have." Snuggling against my chest, she says, "I don't want to go back, Daniel."

"To Hawthorne?"

When she exhales, her warm breath dances across my chest. "To a life without this. I don't want to go back to Hawthorne and pretend I'm not in love with you. But we can't . . ."

"We'll figure it out."

"How?"

I kiss her head and pull her against me, my dick already responding to the feel of her soft body against mine.

"I don't know yet. But we'll figure it out, because I'm not going back, either."

Chapter
TWENTY-EIGHT

A DROP OF sweat trickles down my chest, past the wire a female officer taped to my skin. Here's hoping it's waterproof.

"What's the setup at Dax's apartment?" Sam asks me. "I looked it up and was surprised to see he lives in a brownstone. Is there security? A maid?"

"No." I think back to the nights I spent with him at his renovated historic home. "I mean, yes. There's a security system, so there's no getting in without setting it off. There's a camera at the front door. He checks the monitor before he answers it."

Sam nods and writes something in a notebook. "What about staff? We've got surveillance on him and we know there's no one in there now, but could anyone show up while you're there?"

I furrow my brow. "No one. His cleaning people come while he's at work, and he uses a meal delivery service. He doesn't like people around when he's home."

There are four of us in the back of a white van with tinted windows. It's me, Daniel, Sam, and another detective. I scoot closer to Daniel on our side of the van, my knowledge of Dax's home bringing on a wave of disgust.

"Okay," Sam says, looking surprised. "So it should just be him?"

I shrug. "And possibly whoever he fucked last night."

"A woman has come and gone a couple times since we started surveillance, but she's not there now."

"She's probably not the only one," I mutter.

Sam is mid-smile when he stops to listen to something in his earpiece.

"Our snipers are having trouble getting eyes inside his place," he tells us. "The blinds are all closed."

"I'll be with her." Daniel puts a hand on my knee. It's so big it covers the entire lower half of my thigh.

"We like to have backup," Sam says. He considers for a couple seconds. "We'll go ahead, but don't bring her inside if he's got other people in there. They could drag her into another room, and you wouldn't be able to stop them."

Daniel's laugh is humorless. "No one's taking her, man. Not with me beside her."

Sam meets his gaze seriously. "Be careful. This guy's got no scruples. You're bringing a woman he wants dead into his home. It could turn bad fast."

"I've got it," Daniel says tersely.

"Yeah, because you hunt every weekend," Sam grumbles. "But deer can't fire back."

Daniel ignores him and turns to me. "Are you still sure about this? Because you don't have to do it. I can go in there with a wire and get pretty damn far with what I know."

I put my hand on top of his. "I'm sure. And I'm ready." I look at Sam. "Are you guys ready?"

He nods and looks at Daniel. "Try to get the blinds raised in the room you're in if you can." He looks back and forth between us. "And if you're in trouble, say, 'It's hot in here.' When we hear those words from either of you, we're busting inside the place. So for fuck's sake, don't say that just because it's warm in his house."

Daniel checks the handgun tucked into the front of his jeans. I'm not sure he even slept last night. Every time I woke up and snuggled close to him, his body was tight with tension. His demeanor is cool and confident, though. Probably for my benefit. Daniel always projects calm.

My nerves are on edge for another reason. In a matter of minutes, I'll be seeing Dax again. He wanted me dead and is responsible for Allison's death. It's not that I dread seeing him, just the opposite. I want to hurt him, despite my physical inability to do so. I want to inflict pain on him the moment he opens the door. Whether I can kill him with my bare hands or not, I want to try.

But that's not what I agreed to do. Sam wants me to talk to Dax and hopefully get him to admit to his crimes. At least some of them.

When it's time to step out of the van, I take a deep breath and steel myself. This is my shot. One way or another, I'm getting justice for my sister.

Daniel looks down at me and tugs the baseball hat he gave me a little lower to shield my face.

"Until we're inside, look down at the ground," he says. "And let me do the talking to get us in there, okay?"

I nod and look up at him solemnly. He cups my jawline in his palm, his thumb grazing across my lips.

"I love you," he whispers, the words meant only for me.

"Okay, guys, it's go time," Sam says from inside the van. "Please don't get me fired, Delgado."

Daniel flashes him a slight grin as Sam pulls the van doors closed. Then he takes my hand, and we walk down the street to Dax's apartment. It's morning, so I'm sure he's still asleep. He likes to party into the early morning hours.

When his elegant brownstone comes into view, I look down at the ground, squeezing Daniel's hand for support. My heart is racing with anticipation. If I blow this, I'll never forgive myself.

As we climb the stairs, I think back to the first time Dax brought me here. I had naïve stars in my eyes back then. I feel like I've aged years in the past six months.

I hear the click of Daniel pushing the buzzer. There's no response.

"We know he's in there," Sam says in my ear. Daniel and I both have on earpieces to keep us in touch with Sam. "Keep ringing."

Daniel lays on the buzzer button, not stopping until Dax's sleepy, pissed-off voice responds.

"Who the fuck are you?"

Daniel's response is gruff. "I'm the attorney for a woman you impregnated, Mr. Caldwell. I suggest you let us in, because we have much to talk about."

His lie makes my stomach roll. Thank God it's just a ruse to get us inside.

Dax scoffs into the intercom. "Talk to my attorney."

"I've sent two requests to your attorney and gotten no response," Daniel says tersely. "If you don't speak to us, we're going to meet with a reporter this afternoon."

"I don't give a fuck," Dax says flatly. "I didn't knock anyone up."

"Hopefully, your father and the board of his company won't give a fuck, either," Daniel says. "We'll be seeking a seven-figure settlement."

"Christ," Dax mutters. "Money-grubbing whores. Who is she?"

Daniel shakes his head in disgust. "You know what? I'm not doing this over your intercom. We're leaving."

He takes my arm and we turn.

"No, wait," Dax says, sounding more awake now. "I'll be right down."

"We're in," Daniel murmurs, probably for Sam's benefit.

I let out a shaky breath as we wait, then mentally build up my resolve. This is my chance, and I have to be strong. It's not about me; it's about Allison. I won't do anything stupid and let her down. I'm cool, calm, and collected, just like Daniel.

When I hear the door open, I see Daniel's foot edge into the doorway. Now Dax can't close it.

"Mr. Caldwell," Daniel booms. "Thank you for your time. If we could just come in for a minute—"

"Look at me," Dax orders me. "We're not talking if I never even fucked you."

Oh, you fucked me, Dax. And I'm about to fuck you back.

I raise my face up to look at him.

"Allison?" He stares for a full second and then goes pale, his eyes wide with disbelief. "No, you're . . . *Ava?*" It's all he can do to choke the word out.

Daniel grabs a fistful of his shirt and walks him backward, his other hand pointing his gun at Dax's chest.

"What the fuck is this?" Dax snarls.

Once Daniel has him inside, I follow and close the door.

"This is your due, Dax," I say.

He makes a move to fight Daniel off, but Daniel is bigger and stronger. He shoves Dax against the exposed brick wall of his entryway.

"Make another move, and I'll blow your fucking brains out." He edges closer to Dax's face. "Go ahead, give me a reason to do it, asshole."

Dax raises his hands in the air, his eyes narrowed.

"Ava," he says in a level tone. "Tell your bodyguard this was all just a misunderstanding."

"You sending two men to my apartment to kill me was *not* a misunderstanding."

"I didn't send anyone to kill you. They were just supposed to scare you."

"Bullshit." Tears gather in my eyes as I approach.

"Stay there," Daniel says to me. "Don't come any closer to us."

Dax is still looking at me with disbelief. "I went to your funeral. I paid for your funeral. I fucking saw your body before—"

"You saw my sister," I say bitterly. "Your thugs murdered my twin sister, Allison."

Silence hangs in the air as I wait for him to admit it. I *need* him to admit it, or Sam won't be able to arrest him.

"I just want my book back," he says. "Give me my book, and we can go our separate ways."

"Fuck you. My sister is dead."

The rage inside me is so powerful I can hardly keep it in. I want to hurt him.

"Madeline gave you the book," Daniel says.

Dax looks at him silently for a few seconds. "No, she didn't. I've gone to a lot of fucking trouble to get that book back. I wouldn't have done that if I'd had it this whole time."

"What, like paying off Hawthorne employees to get the information out of the woman you thought was Allison?" Daniel asks.

"Who the fuck's been talking?" Dax demands. "I seem to have a mole." He glares at Daniel. "You get your hands off me, or you won't walk out of this house when we're through."

Daniel slams Dax against the wall again. "I'm gonna ask you some questions. You've got two seconds to answer each one. If three seconds pass, I pull this trigger."

Dax licks his lips nervously. I've never seen him in a subordinate position like this. He was always the one making the rules.

"Did your employee Eli hire a CNA named Eric Hunt and a doctor named Marcia Heaton to get information out of Allison Cole while she was a patient at Hawthorne?"

Eyes narrowed, Dax says, "I don't know the names of the people Eli approached for help, but yes, there were two and one was a female doctor."

"You get to live for at least a few more seconds," Daniel says, the gun still aimed at Dax's chest. "Now, did you hire two men to break in to Ava's apartment in March and kill her?"

Two seconds of silence pass. I don't know if I want Dax to admit it, or if I'd prefer that Daniel kill him. Sam wouldn't be okay with the latter option, but from the vein standing out in Daniel's neck, I feel like he's angry enough to do it.

As Dax opens his mouth to respond, the front door opens. I look over and see Madeline coming inside. She closes the door while looking at her cell phone screen and calls out, "Get naked, baby."

She sees me and stops. Shock sets in, her lips dropping open as she stares at me.

"Ava?"

None of the people who knew Allison and me well enough to tell us apart saw me after she died. I can only imagine that when Dax saw Allison's body, she was in a state that didn't allow him to tell the difference between us, which sickens me. We always wore our hair the same and even shared clothes. It was our voices and mannerisms that set us apart.

Madeline's not the only one who's shocked. I'm still reeling from her "Get naked, baby" comment.

"You're with Dax?" I can barely get the words out.

She knew when I brought her the book that it was about Dax and it was bad. And then I was murdered the next day, or so she thought.

"You're *alive?*" she croaks.

"Mad," Dax says. "A little help here?"

She looks over at him for the first time, and her eyes widen. "What the hell is going on?"

"There's a gun in the desk drawer of my office," Dax says. "Go get it, baby."

She nods numbly and starts to move.

"Don't let that happen, Ava," Daniel says. "Stop her."

"We don't want to hurt you, Madeline," I say. "You need to stay right where you're at."

"Where's the fucking book?" Daniel demands, pressing the gun to Dax's head. "Madeline said she gave it to you."

"She never even had it," Dax says.

Madeline moves to dart past me, and I jump on her, both of us falling to the ground. We wrestle each other for control, hands grabbing and long hair obstructing our vision.

"Stop," I cry. "Dax had Allison murdered. It was supposed to be me, Madeline."

She keeps fighting me, and I realize the news didn't even faze her. Something is very, very wrong here. When she grunts and starts to get the upper hand on me, panic fills my chest. If she gets that gun, things will go to hell.

I grab a handful of her hair and slam her head to the ground, then crawl out from under her and straddle her waist, panting with exertion.

"You *knew*," I say bitterly. I press my knees to the floor and hold her wrists together in front of me. "You fucking knew he tried to kill me."

She fights to regain control, breaking her wrists free. I slap her in the face to daze her, then take hold of her arms again. Betrayal runs hot through my veins, infusing me with newfound strength.

"Dax says she never had the book," Daniel says from several feet away.

"He's lying. I handed it to her in her office the day before Allison was murdered."

"The *fuck*?" Dax yells. "Is that true, Maddie?"

"No, she's making it up," Madeline says, still fighting to break free of my hold.

"Why would I make that up?" I yell in her face. "I told you to keep it safe, and you fucking brought it to him, didn't you? Were you already with him then?"

The hatred I see in her eyes is like a punch to the stomach. Where did it come from?

"Yes, I was with him. I'd been fucking him for a month."

Her vitriolic tone tells me she thinks this news will hurt. It doesn't hurt that Dax did it, but my business partner? My friend?

"Did she give you my book?" Dax demands angrily. "Maddie, if you've got my fucking book, after all the goddamn trouble I've gone through to get it back—"

"I called Dax right after you left my office that day," Madeline says to me.

"Yeah, and you told me she had my book and planned to give it to the cops. You never fucking mentioned that you had it." Dax is way past angry.

"Why?" I keep my voice level, forcing myself not to let the hurt show.

"I didn't want to share Brighton Cole with you anymore. It was supposed to be fifty-fifty, but you wanted to be the star. You were the face of the label. You were a selfish bitch."

Her admission stuns me. She never even hinted at feeling this way in all the time we were business partners.

"I left my half of Brighton Cole to Allison," I say. "You still didn't have control."

Madeline's lips curl into an ugly smile. "Actually, your will allowed me to buy her interest out."

My heart stills in my chest. "It did not."

"Hmm." She arches a brow. "The will was in my safe, Ava. Don't you think I know what it says?"

"You bitch." I tighten my hold on her wrists. "You conniving, evil bitch. You changed my will?"

She holds my gaze, victory written all over her smug face.

"I would've given it to you," I say, my voice breaking with emotion. "All of it. Dax, too. If you had just said . . . Allison meant more to me than the company."

"I didn't know he'd have her killed instead of you," Madeline says dismissively. "Obviously, the guys he hired fucked up."

"Yeah, they did," Dax says darkly. "And they'll pay. But you fucked up, too, Maddie."

"Are you gonna have me killed, too?" She turns to glare at him. "Your stack of bodies is getting pretty tall, Dax. One of these days you'll get busted."

The front door opens with a thud as it slams against the wall. A team of SWAT officers storms inside. There's yelling and commotion, and soon I feel myself being lifted off of Madeline.

Daniel carries me out of the apartment, turning to the side as he walks through the doorway.

"It's over," he says. "Sam got what he needed. It's over now, Ava."

I cry silent tears, both relieved it's over and sad that the betrayal went even deeper than I'd realized. The truth hurts sometimes. This truth hurts so deep I'm not sure it will ever stop.

Chapter
TWENTY-NINE

I EXHALE WITH relief as I walk back into the hotel room. Ava's curled up in a chair, looking lost in thought.

"How'd it go?" she asks, turning to look at me.

"Good." I sit down on the edge of the bed so I'm facing her. My phone call with Joanne Hawthorne had gone much better than expected.

"So you're not fired, then?" She arches her brows hopefully.

"Not fired. And not in trouble with the law."

She smiles. "I'm so glad, Daniel."

I lean forward, resting my elbows on my knees. "Leonard's service was yesterday."

"Oh, no." Ava gets up and sits next to me, wrapping her small arm around my broad back. "I'm sorry we missed that."

I nod. "Leonard would have wanted us to do what we were doing. That's the kind of guy he was. He was cremated, and he asked in his will for me to scatter his ashes in the lake we always fished at. That'll be . . ." I clear away the lump in my throat. "That'll be when I pay my respects to him."

She rubs her palm in circles over my back. "So what else did Joanne say?"

"She's broken up about things. She thinks if she would have listened to me before, Leonard would still be alive."

Ava's "hmm" of sympathy is soft. "I understand exactly how she feels."

I wrap my arms around her and pull her into my lap, holding her close. "I've got regrets, too. If I wasn't a drunk, Michael Trone would still be alive."

"Your patient who died?"

"Yeah. I think about him. What he might have done with his life. Whom he might have influenced or saved. Life's one big row of dominoes, and I took one out of the mix."

Ava puts her head on my shoulder. "After Allison died, I didn't feel like I even deserved to live. Did you go through that, too?"

"Yeah. I had some very dark days in rehab. All that guilt and remorse, and no booze to drown it in."

"But you made it," she says softly. "And then you saved me. So the dominoes of life are still doing their thing."

"I didn't save you."

She sits up and meets my eyes, hers shining with sincerity. "You *did* save me, Daniel. You saw me as a whole, worthy person when no one else did. Not even me. You believed me over Dr. Heaton. You saved me from Eric. When I was most vulnerable, you were there for me."

My heart fills with love for her. "I always will be, Ava. Always. Joanne wants me back at Hawthorne, but I know there's no life for you there. You don't need to be an inpatient at a mental hospital anymore. So if you want to go somewhere new and start fresh . . . together . . ."

The longest second of my life passes as I wait for her response.

"I want to go back to Hawthorne with you. If we can be

together, that's all I need."

"You mean that?"

She smiles. "Of course I do. Hawthorne feels like home to me now. The people there . . . the ones I know, anyway . . . I get them. I know what it's like to feel yourself losing control of your own mind. It's terrifying. Maybe I could be of some help there, somehow. I could work there."

"You're a fashion designer, though."

"Not anymore. I was always a business owner first and foremost, anyway. And I'm damn good at that. Maybe I could do remote business consulting. Or get a counseling license. I just want to do something brand new, with no ties to fashion. This is my fresh start."

She shifts in my lap, straddling me, and I kiss her.

"It's a fresh start for me, too," I say against her lips. "A chance I never thought I'd have again."

"I admire what you do at Hawthorne. They need you."

I slide my hands around her ass, gripping it in my palms. "And I like my work there. But what I need is *you*, so if it ever stops working for you, we'll move on."

"I love the country there. It's like its own world, full of blue skies and new possibilities."

"Possibilities like you having my last name?"

She smiles. "Yes, that's a definite possibility."

I brush a lock of dark hair back from her face. "I'm sorry about Madeline. I know it hurt you."

She sighs softly. "It did. But we did what we came here to do. Dax is in jail, and Madeline will get hers for what she did. I'm fighting to get my share of Brighton Cole back. I'll sell it when I do, because I want nothing to do with that company. But she'll lose; I know that. And I get *you*. I'm ready to let go of the bitterness and live again. Allison would want that." She blinks and a tear slides down her cheek. "You'll think this is crazy, but—"

"No, I won't."

She smiles through her tears. "My eyes locked with Allison's as she was dying. I saw so much in her eyes that was too painful to confront at the time. From the moment she held up her hand with the engagement ring on it, I felt what she was telling me. She willingly took my place. She died for me, and she knew I would have done the same for her. She loved me." Ava wipes her cheeks and takes a breath before continuing. "And she knew how much I loved her. She wanted me to live for both of us. I can't bear the thought of her dying so I could live a miserable life. I want to be happy every day and live to be a hundred years old and tell my grandchildren about my beautiful, brave sister. That's my new dream."

"Then let's make it come true."

She smiles, grabs my face, and leans in to kiss me. "What about you? What's your dream?"

"You."

"You really know how to melt a girl, Dr. Lumberjack."

I squeeze her ass, pulling her against me. "I want to make love to you in front of the fireplace in my cabin, Ava. I want to wake up with you every day for the rest of my life. I want you to know Caleb. I want to deliver our babies. I want to teach our children how to hunt and fish and ride horses. I want us to keep healing each other until the hurt doesn't define either of us anymore."

She nods slightly and puts her arms around my neck, running her fingers up into my hair. "Yes."

"I love the sound of you saying *yes*." I dip my face into her neck to kiss her. She moans softly and grinds against me.

"You're good at making me say it," she says in a sultry tone.

I trace the tip of my tongue over her collarbone. "Was Dax your type before, baby? Did you like your men lean with long hair? The type who hire others to do their dirty work?"

She edges back and looks at me. "Tell me you're not jealous of him, Daniel."

"No. You're mine now. Nothing to be jealous of. I'm just wondering. Have you been with a man like me before?"

Her sexy smile makes my balls ache. "If I'd ever been with an inked-up lumberjack doctor who fucked me into next week and said sweet things in my ear after, I wouldn't be here, would I? That's not the kind of man a girl lets get away."

She tries to push me onto the bed, but I hold her in place. My cock is throbbing, desperate to be inside her.

"You've shown me how assertive you can be in bed, Miss Cole." I pull her hips against me, letting her feel how worked up she's got me. "And I like it. But this time, it's my turn."

She licks her lips, her eyes glazed with lust. "Yes."

"There's my favorite word. Now take your shirt off for me."

She pulls her shirt up over her head, her tits perfect in a pretty white bra. I reach back and pull my own shirt off, tossing it to the floor before I wind a hand around her ponytail and tug it back, opening her neck up to my mouth.

I kiss and nip and lick her skin as she moans for more. Now that we've got everything on the table, I'm feeling possessive of the woman who's not just mine for today, but for all the days to come.

"Get on your knees," I tell her, breathing hard as she scrambles off my lap and gets to her knees in front of me.

She's eager, reaching for my fly before I even say anything. I smile and wrap my hand around her ponytail again, leaning my face down to hers.

"Is there something in my pants you want?"

"Yes."

"Well, it belongs to you, so take it out, baby."

She exhales in a rush, her cheeks flushed as she unbuttons and unzips my pants and takes out my very hard cock. She kisses and licks and sucks until I'm a groaning, frenzied mess of pent-up wanting.

When I can't take it anymore, I tear off the rest of our clothes, tell her to get on her back, and watch her chest rise and fall as I slide a condom on. The orgasm at the end of fucking her always feels amazing, but this moment is a close second. Seeing her desperate and hungry for me gets me going like nothing else.

Her groan is as loud as mine when I slide inside her. I have to get as deep as her tight little body will allow me, but I start slow to make up for it. I spend several blissful minutes pumping in and out of her, the only sounds in the room her moans, my groans, and the slapping together of our bodies.

"Oh, Daniel," she says in a breathy tone. "Just like that. Please don't stop."

Not only don't I stop, I thrust deeper and faster, fueled by her cries of pleasure. Her whole body tenses as she comes with a scream, and I can't hold back any longer. I let myself go, coming harder than I ever have with a hard groan and a shudder.

Ava hums with satisfaction as I lie down. "That was amazing."

"Yeah, it was."

She curls into my side. "Are we leaving tomorrow?"

I sigh heavily. "I could spend a week in this room with you, but . . . we should leave tomorrow. Joanne said Tillman's ready for me to be back."

"We'll leave tomorrow, then. I miss Morgan. I'm looking forward to talking to her for the first time."

"Good luck with that. She tends to dominate conversations."

She laughs, her breath tickling my chest. "That's home, though. I'm ready to leave Chicago behind forever."

"Yeah, I get that." I kiss the top of her head.

"There's somewhere I want to stop on our way out of town, though."

"Where's that?" I ask.

"I'll tell you in the morning. Tonight, I just want . . . this."

"I'll give you as much *this* as your body can handle, baby."

Chapter
THIRTY

AS THE CHICAGO skyline gets smaller, I feel freer. If I ever return to my hometown, it won't be anytime soon.

I wish I could only take the good memories with me, but I have to take them all. I hope the bad ones will fade with time. When I think of Allison, I want to remember us giving each other matching haircuts at age five. The photo Mom took after she stopped crying makes me smile every time I see it. Then there was the time we switched classrooms for a full week in fifth grade because our teachers couldn't tell us apart. Her standing in for me on a date in high school when I had the flu, and the many texts she sent about how it was going.

AVA! You didn't tell me he's nineteen.

He's in college, that's pretty hot.

Am I allowed to make out with him??

"What's funny?" Daniel asks from the driver's seat.

"Just thinking about Allison."

He takes my hand and holds it loosely in his own. It's exactly what I need. I don't want to share the memory, but it's good to have him close and know he cares.

It's late morning, and we're planning to get to Hawthorne early tomorrow. If I know Daniel, he'll still want to round on patients, even after being up all night.

"Do you think Joanne Hawthorne will mind me staying?" I ask. "It's kind of a weird transition to make—patient to . . . whatever I decide to do."

"We're a package deal. And no, she won't mind. She has to pay high salaries to get people to relocate there, so if you decide to get a counseling license, she'll hire you."

I laugh at the image. "Once I clear a psych evaluation. Wouldn't it be weird for the patients to have a former patient as their counselor?"

"I don't think so. You're proof that recovery is possible. And like you said, you get them."

I sigh softly. "I'm not sure I'd be a good counselor. And if I had to work with someone like Dr. Heaton—"

"She was fired," Daniel says. "Her medical license is suspended pending an investigation."

"She admitted what she did?"

"Under police questioning. That's what Joanne told me."

I shake my head and look out the passenger side window as the cemetery sign comes into view.

"People like her shouldn't become doctors," I say sadly. "Why would she do something so awful? Trying to make me break when I was still grieving?"

"Apparently, her son has heavy gambling debts, and she took the money to help him. Not that it justifies what she did."

"No, it doesn't."

He brings my hand to his lips and kisses it. "I'll do the recruiting for the next psychiatrist. I'll make sure we get someone great."

As he drives through the open wrought-iron gates at the

cemetery's entrance, Daniel looks up at the oak trees that tower over the property.

"This place is beautiful," he says. "Those trees have to be more than a century old."

"It's a hidden gem. My grandparents bought several plots here many years ago. They're all sold now."

"Are they still around? Your grandparents?"

I shake my head. "It's just me and my aunt Maggie. I need to call her when we get back to Hawthorne and explain everything."

"What happened to your parents?"

"My dad died in a car accident when Allison and I were young. And Mom died of ovarian cancer three years ago."

"I'm sorry."

I squeeze his hand. "What about your parents?"

"They have a place in Spain where they're living now. I'd like to take you there to meet them sometime soon."

I half smile and half cringe. "I don't have Allison's passport, and I'm not sure I should try to use my own."

"Sam said he'll help us get things straightened out." He lowers his brows with concern. "But you should know . . . the authorities may want to exhume Allison's body."

My stomach rolls at the thought. "I really hope they don't."

"I know. Me too. We'll just have to see."

I point at the fork in the road ahead of us. "Turn right up there."

It's been a while since I was here. It's comforting to know I can come visit my parents' graves anytime I want to. Just knowing they have a place that will always belong to them means everything, whether I come here often or not.

The hydrangeas next to my mom's headstone are in full bloom. As soon as Daniel parks the truck, I get out and walk over to the soft, pale pink flowers.

"These were her favorite," I say to Daniel as he approaches. "Allison and I planted them."

I look at my mom's headstone and then at my dad's, hoping it'll give me strength. It doesn't help much, though. I'm still filled with cold dread as I walk over to the headstone next to my dad's.

Daniel stands behind me, his hands on my shoulders as I take in a deep breath and raise my eyes to look at it.

Ava Eleanor Cole
Beloved daughter, sister, and friend

It's surreal seeing my name on a headstone. It sends a chill down my spine, despite the humid August air.

"I'm going to have one made for her," I murmur. "She doesn't even have something with her own name on it to tell the world she was here."

My throat constricts and tears brim in my eyes. Daniel is silent behind me. I put my hand over one of his on my shoulder.

"I don't feel close to her because the stone is wrong," I say.

I move to the fresh, bright green patch of grass in front of the headstone and get on my knees, putting my palms on the ground. Closing my eyes, I let the unshed tears slide down my cheeks.

"I love you so much. You're the other half of me, Allie. I never thought I'd have to do anything without you, and now . . . I have to do *everything* without you."

A soft breeze ruffles the leaves on the oak tree towering above us. Daniel's boots crunch in the gravel as he walks away to give me time alone with my sister.

Despite all the times I've wished I could talk to her since she died, I like these moments of quiet. The breeze keeps blowing, and the scent of Mom's hydrangeas floats through the air. With my hands on this grass, I have a sense of closeness to Allison that I never thought I'd feel again.

I'd give the breath from my own lungs to bring her back. If I could only trade places with her right now so she could be the one with a beautiful life still in front of her, I would.

But this is all I can do. I can cherish her in my heart every day and live a life that honors her sacrifice. I silently vow to her that I'll laugh as often as possible. I'll be daring. I'll be strong and brave. All the things that she was, I'll be, too.

I press my cheek to the grass, my eyes still closed. After a few seconds, I get back on my knees and press a kiss to my palm, then put my hand on the grass.

"I'll be back," I whisper. "I'll plant roses here for you. Pink ones, like that corsage you got before prom and saved forever."

Then I wipe my cheeks, stand up, and take a deep breath. Daniel is walking down the gravel path, and I catch up to him.

"You can stay as long as you like," he says, looking down at me.

"I'm good."

He wraps his arms around me, and I sink against him, his solid strength reassuring me.

"I love you, Ava Eleanor Cole."

"And I love you, Daniel . . . what's your middle name?"

He hums with amusement. "Joseph."

"Daniel Joseph Delgado."

"Are you ready to go home?"

I look up at him and smile. "I'm ready."

EPILOGUE

Three years later

GRACIE BURIES HER chubby little fingers in the soil next to mine. She likes the cool, fresh feel of earth as much as I do.

"Dig, Mommy," she says with a grin.

I kiss the top of her cute little nose. "I am, sweets. I'm pulling weeds."

No matter how much things grow and change, weeding the garden is still one of my favorite things to do. Pulling weeds is therapeutic, and I like seeing the thriving gardens neat and clean.

Leonard left a substantial sum of money to Hawthorne, and Joanne Hawthorne used it to create the Leonard Harris Memorial Garden. His tomato garden was expanded, and other vegetables were planted. I often look out over the rows of plants and neat, raised wood beds and smile, thinking about how much Leonard would love this.

There's a colorful flower garden with brick paths, benches, and a gazebo, but I spend most of my time in the vegetable gardens. I helped plan and plant them, and while I was pregnant with Gracie,

I harvested vegetables and worked with the Hawthorne chef to perfect a spaghetti sauce recipe using the tomatoes we grow.

The chef, Mario, is Italian, so that project was a labor of love. We developed a recipe, and he started using it for meals at Hawthorne Hill. When we began canning it for winter, Hawthorne staffers started asking to buy it. That was when I asked Caleb during a Skype session if he would color a label for me. He did, and I added the name Leonard's Garden Sauce to it, then printed the labels and added them to the jars so they'd have some flair.

Leonard's Garden Sauce took off like I never could have imagined. Word spread, and soon I was filling orders for the hardware store in Greenville to sell to their customers. When I couldn't keep up on my own anymore, I set up shop in an empty staff cabin, and Daniel convinced Joanne to let me hire some Level One patients to help with the business. We've kept growing since.

"'Mato," Gracie says, pulling a plump, red fruit from a vine and holding it up proudly.

She'll be two in a couple months, and Daniel and I adore her. So does Caleb. He started spending more time with us after we got married almost three years ago. The older he gets, the more he looks like Daniel.

We were married right here, on the bluff that overlooks the lush green valley below. I never would have imagined a wedding on the grounds of a mental hospital could be perfect, but it was. Hawthorne is no average hospital, and Daniel is most certainly no average man. He promised me everything he is and ever will be.

I don't believe all things happen for a reason. I don't think Allison was murdered and Daniel delved down a destructive path of alcoholism so we could both end up at Hawthorne and meet. But as I looked up into his dark, beautiful eyes that day, I knew the woman who once accepted a marriage proposal from Dax Caldwell had no idea there was a man like Daniel out there. A strong man whose shoulders are broad in every way. I fall more in love with him every day, and though tragedy brought us together, we move forward together. He picks me up when I fall.

No amount of money or connections could save Dax from prison. Once I knew he was behind bars for at least the next couple of decades, I put him out of my mind. He doesn't deserve a place in my memory.

My family has helped me find peace, and though the hole in my heart will never be gone, it gets smaller with time. My love for Gracie reminds me of my love for Allison—pure and unconditional. As she grows, I'm reminded that life continues.

Brody Tillman works closely with Daniel now so Daniel can have time off. He takes two days a week just for our family. We hike in the woods with Gracie in a carrier on Daniel's back, and we camp with her nestled in between us. Those are my favorite times.

"Put that tomato in your basket," I tell my daughter. She toddles off to get the small wicker basket she carries around the gardens.

Everyone here loves her. For people with such small biological families, Daniel and I are able to surround our daughter with love. We're careful not to expose her to anything she's too young for, but it's also important to us that she knows people with mental illnesses are people just like everyone else. The patients who work for me sometimes spend time laughing and coloring with her while I'm crunching numbers nearby, and though it's untraditional, for us, it works.

Leonard's Garden Sauce was just the start of something big. When Gracie was old enough for solid foods, I pureed vegetables from the garden, making my own organic baby food. Just like with the sauce, the baby food was soon in demand.

Last year, I started Allie Bee, my organic baby food company. Allison's middle name was Beatrice, and Dad called her Allie Bee when we were little. It was the perfect name for my business.

Allie Bee is booming, and we quickly outgrew the cabin Joanne was letting us use. I had a new log building constructed near the gardens for the manufacturing operations. Fortunately, Hawthorne has unlimited outdoor space. Joanne had our new family cabin built near the Allie Bee shop. She's still wooing Daniel with perks, always worried he'll leave Hawthorne. But this is our home. We travel to Spain a few times a year to see his parents, but it always feels good to get back to the big sky country of Montana.

"Daddy!" Gracie squeals. She runs toward him, tomatoes bouncing out of her basket on the way.

Daniel bends down and scoops her up, his adoration for our daughter written on his face. "How's my girl?"

"I got 'mato," Gracie says, looking in the basket and frowning at its emptiness.

Daniel points at the tomatoes she dropped, and she scrambles out of his arms to retrieve them.

"Are you on lunch?" I ask him, standing up and brushing my hands off on my shorts.

"I am." He comes over and kisses me. "Mario made us lunch to eat in the gazebo."

"That sounds nice. I'll go wash my hands."

When I walk into the gazebo a few minutes later, Daniel's white coat is folded over an empty chair and Gracie is helping him take food out of a picnic basket.

"How's your day?" Daniel asks me.

"It's good. I just got a big order from a grocery store chain."

He grins. "A grocery store chain? That's great, babe."

"It is. I'm happy about it, but Morgan's gonna blow a gasket when I tell her. She's already stressed."

Morgan is my operations manager. She oversees the production side of Allie Bee, and she's very good at it. She's a lot like me—driven to do well because it feels good, not because she needs the money. Milo was only here for six months before getting discharged, and I know she still misses him. They write letters, but it's not the same as seeing him every day.

Madeline avoided jail time by testifying against Dax. She paid a price, though, when I won a large legal settlement from her over Brighton Cole. I offered to sell her the company, but she couldn't afford it due to the settlement. We sold it to a big label, and I did well on that, too. Money will never be a worry for us, and for that, I'm grateful. But we don't want Gracie to grow up surrounded by material things. Everything we really need, we had in the small, cozy cabin we lived in before Joanne had our new one built.

We would have needed more space eventually, so I'm grateful for our new home. Now Caleb has his own room when he comes to stay with us, and we have room for more kids.

"I think Morgan thrives on stress," Daniel says, handing Gracie a small section of a cheese sandwich.

I laugh, agreeing with him. Morgan and the other patients who work for me would do it for free, but I'd never allow that. They like having a job to go to and a purpose. Ty, the new psychiatrist Daniel recruited and hired, spends time in the shop every day, just talking and making sure everyone's doing well.

The only price Dr. Heaton paid for her wrongs was the loss of her medical license. But since that means she can't see patients anymore, it's enough for me. What happened with her seems so long ago now.

After we're finished eating, one of the nurses comes to the gazebo and asks if she can take Gracie to walk in the gardens. Gracie goes happily, her basket in hand.

I'm packing up the last of our lunch when Daniel gets up from his side of the table and walks over to me.

"Leave that, babe. I'll get it."

"I don't mind."

He smiles and wraps an arm around my waist, pulling me close. "You take such good care of us."

I nestle against his chest, taking in his faint, spicy cedar scent. "You take good care of me back."

"I talked to my mom earlier. I was thinking next month we could take the kids to Spain for a week and let my parents hang with them while we spend some time in Formentera."

"Ohh." I look up at him with a wide smile.

"Yeah." He nods and arches his brows. "What better place to get busy making the next baby than our honeymoon spot, right?"

I sigh happily. "Work is crazy busy, but I can't say no to that. I'll figure it out. Let's go."

He kisses me, the brush of his stubble against my skin still making my stomach flutter. "My parents will be thrilled."

"I'm all for Formentera and baby-making, but you should know . . ."

Daniel furrows his brow and studies my expression. "What, babe? Everything okay?"

A smile spreads across my face. "I think I may already be pregnant."

His eyes shine with happiness. "Yeah?"

"I mean, it's early, but . . . I'm late. I ordered some tests."

"I've got some in my supply room." He takes my hand and leads me toward the main lodge. "Let's go do one."

I laugh at his enthusiasm. "But it's still early."

"As long as you're late, we're good."

I call out to the nurse walking with Gracie and ask her to keep an eye on her for a few minutes. She says she's happy to, and I stop Daniel so we can get the lunch basket and his white coat from the gazebo.

"If I am pregnant, do you still want to go to Formentera?" I ask him.

"Yeah, definitely. We'll have something to celebrate, then. Either way, you won't need to pack many clothes."

He gives me a sexy grin as he puts his white coat back on over his polo, takes the basket with one hand and my hand with his other, and heads toward the lodge, his strides so big and fast I have to run to keep up.

My heart is hammering, and it's not from our pace. It's because not only am I alive, I'm in love with my life. It's everything Allison would have wanted for me, and so much more.

ABOUT THE AUTHOR

BRENDA ROTHERT LIVES in Central Illinois with her husband and three sons. She was a daily print journalist for nine years, during which time she enjoyed writing a wide range of stories.

These days Brenda writes Contemporary Romance. She loves to hear from readers.

CONNECT WITH BRENDA

www.brendarothert.com

Facebook

Twitter

Goodreads

Pinterest

BOOKS BY
BRENDA ROTHERT

NOW SERIES
Now and Then
Now and Again
Now and Forever

FIRE ON ICE SERIES
Bound
Captive
Edge
Drive
Release

ON THE LINE SERIES
Killian
Bennett
Liam (coming soon)

LOCKHART BROTHERS SERIES
Deep Down
In Deep
Drawn Deeper
Hidden Depth (coming soon)

STANDALONES
Unspoken
Barely Breathing
Blown Away
Dirty Work (with Chelle Bliss)
His
Hooked

ACKNOWLEDGEMENTS

I'VE WANTED TO write a book about twin sisters for a while now, but I couldn't come up with a story line I was excited about. That is, until the idea for this one hit. From the moment I started thinking about this story, I knew it would require more planning and plotting than I typically do. That process was surprisingly fun.

Two amazing friends helped with this book from those beginning stages. Janett Gomez read it chapter by chapter, her feedback helping steer my writing. Stephanie Reid read the open and then had an epic brainstorming session with me at Panera that helped me fill in all the plot holes. There would be no Come Closer without the two of them, and I love them so much.

I was inspired during the planning stages by the photo I bought from Sara Eirew for the cover. She also worked tirelessly on the design for the cover—twice. The first time I came up with ideas for the design that just didn't work out. The second time I let her do what she does best and she rocked it.

Editor Lisa Hollett made this story better, as always. Copy Editor Taylor Bellitto ironed out all my mistakes, and Joanne Thompson did a great job on the final proofread.

The rest of my beta reading team is Chelle Northcutt/M.E. Carter, Chantal Gemperle and Michelle Tan. They all read this book at different stages of completion to help me make sure I wasn't ruining any of the plot turns. They're the best team I could ask for.

My formatter and interior designer, Christine Borgford, helped make this book beautiful. It meant everything to work with her on this book, because she puts passion and creativity into her work, and that's what I wanted for Come Closer.

There are so many authors, bloggers and readers who made this book possible. Thank you all for your friendship and support.

I hope I kept you guessing with this story, readers, and I hope I surprised you in places. But more importantly, I hope you take away from this story that we sometimes never recover fully from the losses of those we love. We move forward to honor them and we learn to smile and feel hopeful again. We're grateful we knew and loved them. But never feeling quite the same after a deep loss is okay. Asking for help to grieve those losses is okay, too, as is seeking help for mental illness. There is goodness out there. If you need it, reach for it, and don't stop reaching until you find it.

www.ingramcontent.com/pod-product-compliance
Lightning Source LLC
Chambersburg PA
CBHW060212180626
46813CB00007B/2795